DESPERATION

BOOK I OF THE ISLAND TRILOGY

C.B. STONE

C.B. Stone Books
www.CBStoneBooks.com

Copyright © 2015 by InkedPlot Media
Copyright © 2015 by Author C.B. Stone

Cover Art by Kellie Dennis at Book Cover by Design
www.bookcoverbydesign.co.uk
Cover photo by Shutterstock

InkedPlot Media
8369 NW 66 ST 7338
Miami, FL 33166

Disclaimer:

This is a work of fiction. Names, characters, businesses, places, events and incidents are either the products of the author's imagination or used in a fictitious manner. Any resemblance to actual persons, living or dead, or actual events is purely coincidental.

Printed in the United States of America.

BOOKS BY C.B. STONE

~Absence of Song Trilogy~

Awakening
http://www.cbstonebooks.com/book/awakening/

Becoming
http://www.cbstonebooks.com/book/becoming/

Chosen
http://www.cbstonebooks.com/book/chosen/

~Unbelief Trilogy~

Rehabilitation
http://www.cbstonebooks.com/book/rehabilitation/

Ruin
http://www.cbstonebooks.com/book/ruin/

Revelation
http://www.cbstonebooks.com/book/revelation/

~The Island Trilogy~

Desperation
http://www.cbstonebooks.com/book/desperation/

Escalation
http://www.cbstonebooks.com/book/escalation/

Deliverance
http://www.cbstonebooks.com/book/deliverance/

Please visit *http://www.CBStoneBooks.com* for the most up-to-date information on books by C.B. Stone, including new releases and current up-coming release dates.

Or subscribe by email and get them right to your inbox:

http://www.CBStoneBooks.com/Subscribe-for-Updates/

Dedicated to all of the believers in the world who don't try to pervert God and a belief in Him into something ugly and fanatical, thereby causing others to blaspheme His name.

Romans 2:23 You who boast in the law dishonor God by breaking the law. 24 For, as it is written, "The name of God is blasphemed among the Gentiles because of you."

One of God's greatest commandments is:
"Love Thy Neighbor"

Luke 10:26 Jesus replied, "What does the law of Moses say? How do you read it?" 27 The man answered, "'You must love the LORD your God with all your heart, all your soul, all your strength, and all your mind.' And, 'Love your neighbor as yourself.'"

May we *all* love others as we love ourselves, and be His hands and feet in the world, spreading salt and light as we strive to illuminate darkness.- Stone

DESPERATION

My lawyer paces in front of the courtroom, clearly passionate in his defense of me. A good thing as far as defenses go, but I'm not really sure why he's so invested, considering he's only a public defender. They aren't known for being well paid in exchange for their toils.

"Your honor, I ask that you consider granting some leniency here. My client has had a very difficult childhood, with more hard knocks than any kid should be forced to endure. She's had no real role models or examples, no steady forces in her life. It's understandable that she has found herself in the position she's in right now, but I believe we have an opportunity here to give her a chance make better choices from here on out, and to prove herself to be a contributing member of society."

The judge steeples his fingers together and stares down over the top of his glasses, pursing his lips and studying me.

I resist an urge to slide down deeper in my seat, or tilt my face forward and hide behind my curtain of hair. He's the sort who makes you feel about 5 years old with just a look. Which I guess is good if you're a judge, but it's not exactly comfortable when you're not.

Instead I remain sitting tall, keeping my shoulders straight and my head back. I can't help the tiny lift of my chin, revealing my detrimental stubborn streak that always seems to get me into hot water. It doesn't seem to be failing me this time.

The judge rumbles, his voice stern with a slight rasp to it. I idly wonder if he's a smoker. *Nah. Too straight-laced.*

"Young lady, you have been charged and found guilty of Possession with Intent to Distribute. This is a very serious crime. Do you understand the nature of the position you have put yourself in?" I swallow, then nod my head. "Yes sir, I understand." I meet his gaze squarely, trying my best to hide the flash of anger and indignation that rises when I hear his words. *That "I" put myself in.* I stifle a snort.

The judge drops his hands down to his podium with a sigh, staring down at the stack of papers in front of him, before speaking again. "Due to the nonviolent nature of the crime and your clean criminal history, I'm going to cut you a little slack. I feel like you're headed down a bad road, but it's not too late for you to change course with the right environment. To that end, I'm sentencing you to 16 months at the Grandy Island Reintegration Camp. This facility is designed to treat and rehabilitate teens and young adults who are considered "at risk", which I believe to be the case with you. Given the right incentives and guidance, it's my hope that I won't find you in my courtroom again. Your lawyer can provide you with further details before processing."

"But your Honor-" my lawyer tries to protest before the judge lifts a hand, interrupting him, "Mr. Bailey, I've made my ruling." He looks down at me. "Do you have anything else to say on this matter Miss Rykehart?"

I stare at him sullenly for a few seconds before I drop my gaze and shrug, muttering, "Yeah. No good deed."

I look back up to see the judge's lips tighten before he picks up his gavel and slams it down with a thunk. "Very well. Court adjourned."

Pacing the holding room I've been placed in while my paperwork is processed, I can't help but be a little nervous. I've never heard of the Grandy Island Reintegration camp, but it sure as heck doesn't sound like a place I want to be.

Rubbing my sweaty palms against my pants, I'm grateful I at least got to change out of that wretched uniform they make you wear. I feel so much more myself in my worn jeans and black tank top. Better able to cope with whatever's coming next, if that makes any sense. I snort. *Pretty sure it doesn't, Reagan.*

I look up and stop pacing as the door opens and my lawyer appears. He motions me forward. "C'mon. The car is ready."

Taking a deep breath, I stand there for a moment, staring at him. Firming my lips, I give a sharp nod, and push myself forward, walking to the door and heading out down the grim looking hallway that is the Miami-Dade County Courthouse.

I can hear him pacing behind me as we make our way out of the building, and pile into the car that's set to take me to my new future. My new life. If you can call it that. Thinking back to what got me here, covering for Claire's lying little butt, I grimace, sighing heavily as I push up against the door and stare out the window, sullen and silent. *Good going, Reagan.*

My lawyer glances my way, a look of what I can only term pity on his face. I glare at him before turning my attention back to the window.

"I'm sorry I couldn't get the sentence reduced, Reagan. Grandy Island is no picnic, I really did my best."

I shrug. Softening somewhat, I look his way again. "You tried, Dave. That's all anyone can ask for." I try to console him, despite the fact that it's *me* facing a bleak stint on some godforsaken island somewhere. I can't help it though. It's the way I'm wired. I slump back deeper into my seat, settling in for the long ride down to the waterfront.

Standing with Dave at the edge of the pier, I stare up at the big ship that's going to transport me to my own personal hell. I swallow hard, refusing to allow the anxiety and fear tying my stomach in knots to show on my face. A girl has to have some pride.

I offer Dave my hand, and he shakes it, before apologizing again. "I'm sorry, Reagan. I really am. Just keep your head down kid, do as your told, and follow orders. Stay out of trouble and maybe I can get you out of there early for good behavior."

Yeah, right. I make a face and swing my backpack over my shoulder, before offering Dave a tight smile. "Thanks Dave. See ya around sometime."

I make my way up the ship's gangway, stopping to allow a guard in uniform check my paperwork and stamp my hand. He grunts, then waves me on. There are about 15 other people, all around my age or slightly older, boarding along with me. *Yay. It's gonna be a party.*

When I reach the deck, we're all herded into a holding area with chairs set up, and bottles of water set out. I mentally sneer. *Why yes, mustn't let the prisoners get dehydrated.*

The captain of the ship appears, speaking over a megaphone. "Listen up folks. We're heading out in about 10 minutes. Find a seat. Make yourself comfortable. The journey is about 3 hours. There's water available for those of you who may be thirsty, and we will be providing dinner about midway through the trip. We will reach the island after nightfall. I'd highly encourage you to be on your best behavior for this excursion, because your actions will be reported to your overseeing officer once you make it to Grandy Island." He glances around, taking a moment to look each of us in the eye meaningfully.

I shift in the uncomfortable chair I'd commandeered when hustled on board, and drop my gaze. Better that than allow him to glimpse any hint of rebellion on my face. *Best behavior gets you nowhere, Reagan.* The silent reminder is truthful, but stings nonetheless.

Another prisoner plops down in a chair next to mine with a huff. His hair is dirty blonde, a tad too long, and stringy. He looks over at me with a grin. "First time headed to Grandy Island?"

I slide my eyes in his direction, keeping my expression bored. "Yep."

He lets out a bark of laughter. "Awesome, a noob."

I glance at him, lifting a brow. "And?"

The guy shrugs. "Nothin', you're just in for a treat's all. Know anything about Grandy Island?"

I shake my head, my curiosity piqued in spite of myself. "Why... what do you know about it? You've been there before?"

The man's lips twist. "Yeah, I've been there. More times than I care to count. It definitely ain't no fancy rehab center, like they try to play it off as on paper."

He leans in closer, lowering his voice. His eyes have a feverish sheen to them, and his breath is sour. I resist an urge to recoil. "It's more like a freakin' concentration camp. A hellhole, where inmates toil in the sun for hours on end."

He shakes his head. "Trust me, it's *misery*. Hard physical labor, and sometimes, the labor doesn't even make sense. Serves no purpose. Like, you have to work your *ass* off just to make clothes and food for everyone living there, but then you're also made to dig and refill holes, for no apparent reason. Break down and rebuild stone walls. It's... I dunno... modern day torture or something."

I swallow hard, squirming in my chair as I stare at him.

I'm sure incredulousness is written all over my face, but I don't care. *This dude is crazy.* No way could this "reintegration camp" be anything like that. It sounds downright medieval.

The guy leans back in his chair and flips his hair out of his eyes, a smirk on his face. "You'll see."

My mind starts racing as I begin picturing all sorts of wacky scenarios in my head about where I'm going and what life there will be like. The minutes tick by, turning into an hour. Which means we're an hour closer to Grandy Island. I look at the ragtag bunch spread out in chairs around me, and feel a surge of panic.

I can't do this. I can't go to this place. I can't go to this... this... little island of horrors. If what this guy says is true, I can't do it.

I glance around the ship, noting the guards patrolling the perimeter of where we're all sitting. We're allowed to get up and move around, we just can't go beyond the guards. As I watch, a girl stands up and walks over to one of them, and he points her down a hallway behind him. *Except when we have to use the bathroom, apparently.*

I watch the girl disappear into the darkness, and a flash just beyond her catches my eye. Looking out over the railing of the ship, I realize the flashing I see is lights in the distance. We must be passing another island or something. If I can see lights, that must mean we aren't too far from the shoreline.

I leap to my feet, mind racing, as I give a nod to the man

sitting next to me who so kindly shared his tale of woe. I grab my backpack, draping it over my shoulder. My forehead is damp with cold sweat, and my heart pounds like it's going to bust out of my chest, but I don't care. I have to find a way off this boat.

Calming myself and arranging my features into some semblance of, I don't know, *not panic*, I approach the guard.

Clearing my throat, I ask, "Sir, may I use the restroom?"

The guard glances at me, clearly bored, and nods. "Sure. It's down the hall, to the right. Make it quick though, I don't want to have to come looking for you." He gives me the requisite stern look, before pointing in the direction of the bathroom.

Swallowing hard, I nod. "Sure, no problem, I'll be fast." I shift my backpack, and the guard puts a hand up. "Wait a minute. What do you need your back pack for if you're just going to the restroom?" He squints at me suspiciously.

I shrug, remaining nonchalant as possible. "Umm... you know... girl stuff." I give him a pointed look, and then glance down my belly.

The guard flushes crimson, and backs up a hasty step. "Oh, I see. Right. Okay, yeah, no problem. Like I said, right down the hall, to your right. Make it quick."

I nod again, ducking my head and letting my long dark hair hide the small grin I can't keep from breaking across my face. I shoulder past him and make my way down the hall, mentally gearing myself up for what I'm going to do next.

Looking behind me, I check to make sure the guard isn't watching as I make my way down the hall, and hang a right. Then I pick up the pace, following the hallway past the bathroom, right around to the other side of the ship. Thankfully it's not a huge vessel, or my reckless plan would never work.

The wind whips at my hair as I step close to the railing and grip it, staring down at the dark water churning below. I take a deep breath, questioning myself. *Reagan, maybe you need to think on this a bit more.*

I shake my head. There's no time. We're already halfway to Grandy Island. If I'm going to make a move, it has to be now, before those lights I saw a few minutes ago fade to oblivion. Tightening the straps of my pack around my shoulders so it's snug, I look around once more, making sure no one is nearby.

Gingerly, I begin to climb up onto the rail. My foot slips and I almost fall, eliciting a surge of terror. Gasping, fingers wrapped around the iron railing in a death grip, I inhale a few deep breaths, soothing myself.

Easy, girl. You want to jump so you can make it away from the boat, not fall and bonk your head so you wind up shark bait.

Taking another bracing breath, I navigate over the rail and balance carefully against the iron. I hesitate one more second before closing my eyes and leaping into the murky darkness below. Eyes squeezed tight, I try not to scream as I drop through blackness.

Suddenly water closes over my face, stealing the breath from my lungs. I choke, and start kicking, hard, instinctively propelling myself away from the churning water frothing in the wake of the small ship.

Frantically, I kick my feet, trying to propel myself up, straining toward air. *Drowning would not be good.* After a few seconds that feel more like hours, I break the surface with a gasp, gulping in giant lungfuls of oxygen as I kick harder and start using my arms to swim. My backpack feels like dead weight on my back, but I'm loath to ditch it. Even though everything will be a soggy mess, it's really all I've got.

Determined, I kick harder, pumping my arms and pushing myself through the warm water with every ounce of strength I can muster.

Please God, don't let there be any sharks looking for dinner, I pray silently.

Then I push fear of the deep unknown back, chalking it up as an unnecessary focus that's only going to freak me out if I keep thinking about it. Bobbing along the surface of the water, I keep my head tilted skyward and make my way around the back end of the ship. My goal is to, *God willing*, reach the lights I estimate to be about a mile and a half away.

Swimming hard, fighting the strong current paired with lazy swells, I start panting. Exhaustion is wearing me down. I glare up at the night sky, sprinkled with cheerful stars as I engage in a battle against the sea.

What the heck were you thinking, Reagan, you big

dummy? The mental chiding doesn't make me feel any better. It's clear I vastly underestimated just how difficult it would be to jump *off* a ship and then swim to shore.

Flipping over on my back, I float for a few minutes, still kicking in the general direction of the lights, but with less vigor. Staring up at the speckled, moonlit sky, I can't help but appreciate the beauty, even if it does feel as though it's mocking me right now.

The moonlight flashes in the whitecaps of the waves, and despite my rising fear, it's almost peaceful this far out. Then the word shark invades my head again. I resume kicking faster and use my arms to windmill me in the direction of shore, my backpack serving as a floaty of sorts.

It feels marginally easier to swim this way, so I stick with it, clenching my jaw in sheer stubbornness, refusing to stop kicking. My legs quiver from exertion, and my arms ache, but I grit my teeth and ignore all of it. At least my stubborn streak is good for something.

After awhile, I'm so focused I don't even realize I'm nearly there, until suddenly I think I feel sand beneath my feet. I gasp and flip back over on my stomach, waiting for the current swell to abate while I feel around with my toes.

Yes! I can feel sand! Looking up, I see lights flickering

closer now. I hold my breath and sink underwater. Digging my toes into the ground for traction, I push myself forward, breaking through the water, then sinking and doing it again, pushing myself closer and closer to the beach's edge with every leap forward.

I do this over and over, using the momentum to shove myself through the churning water. It's something I used to do as a kid for fun, but this time it's literally saving my life.

The water pours off of me as the waves get shallower and shallower, now crashing around my hips rather than swelling.

Slogging through the waves, I flip my backpack off and drag it behind me, first stumbling and then all but crawling the rest of the way to the shore. Head down, my hair a sodden sheet tangling around my arms, I fumble forward, face planting on the edge of the beach, water flooding up my nose.

I choke a mouthful of salty sea. Out of nowhere strong hands grip my arms, and yank me upright out of the waves. I spit sand and water out of my mouth, coughing. Dazed, I look up, water streaming from my eyes, the sting of salt making them burn. I can just make out the shape of a man, wearing what appears to be a uniform.

Oh no! All that work and you've been found already? Good going, Reagan!

The man half drags, half carries me the rest of the way

out of the waves, before letting me go. Once on dry land, I collapse, chest heaving, panting, every muscle in my body quivering with fatigue. The stranger reaches out as though to help me up, and I wave him away, trying to recover my breath.

Before I manage to fully catch it, he all but bellows in my ear, "What the hell do you think you're *doing*? Are you flippin' *crazy* or something?"

My chest heaves. Hunched over and still spitting gritty sand from my mouth, I shove my hair aside to glare up at him. The moonlight has become so bright it could almost be daytime, so I have no trouble seeing him clearly once the water is gone from my eyes.

Looking him over, I notice he's definitely wearing a uniform, but not like the kind the guards on the ship were wearing.

I frown. No, this uniform is kind of odd, really. Like a cross between an altar-boy and a cop or soldier or something. I wrinkle my nose, trying to make out the word embroidered across the front. Squinting, I can just barely see what looks like Drake spelled out.

My gaze shooting daggers at odds with my tone, very gently I inform him, "I'm right here next to you, buddy. You don't have to yell. And no, I am not *crazy*. I'm desperate, there is a difference."

Climbing slowly to my feet, I realize once standing that

Drake or whoever he is, is pretty dang tall. I'm no slouch my-self at 5'8 but he towers at least a good 4 or 5 inches over me.

My belly does a tiny little somersault when I notice how handsome he is. Clearly strong, if his grip on me had been anything to go by, lean and muscular, with white-blonde hair. I can't quite make out the color of his eyes in the moon-light, but I can see that whatever color they are, they are bright and beautiful.

Why do men always get the pretty eyes? I grump to my-self. And considering he lives on an island, he's probably rocking a year round tan.

I grimace. He's the total antithesis to my long dark hair and moss green eyes, pale skin and slim frame. The only thing in the looks department we *do* have in common is our above average height. And considering the way he's current-ly glaring back at me, clearly the belly twisting somersaults I'm experiencing in reaction to him are not reciprocated.

"Desperate, why? What in *God's good name* possessed you to jump off a ship into the middle of the freakin' *ocean*? And after dark, no less?"

Trying to wring some of the water out of my hair and my clothes, I glance up at him, ignoring his question. "Am I on Grandy Island?"

The man I think is named Drake looks confused. "Grandy Island? Never heard of it. You're on Halcyon Island right now."

I frown. Well, at least that answers one question. Thank God I didn't inadvertently land myself on Grandy. Thinking fast, I nod, trying to come up with a story that will sound plausible. If this Drake guy has never heard of Grandy Island, I certainly don't want to tell him my full story. I have no idea if he will feel compelled to report me or what.

He shifts impatiently. "So why so desperate? What made you jump off a ship?"

I shrug, the fib tripping off my tongue more easily than I expected, "I didn't exactly jump. I was on a cruise ship, and being dumb, I fell overboard, and the only thing I knew to do was swim for the lights that I could see."

Drake looks skeptical. "Fell off a cruise ship? That doesn't explain desperate."

I snort. "Well obviously you've never fallen off a ship before, now have you? Dark, murky, possibly shark infested waters suddenly closing over your head can have a pretty desperate effect on a body."

I think I see the ghost of a smile cross his lips before it's gone, like it never was. *Great, the man finds me amusing.*

Even more annoyed now, I demand, "Look, thanks for dragging me the rest of the way out of the water. Do you think you can take me to someone with some authority around here? Someone who might be able to help me out or something?"

My tone must offend him, because annoyance and

surprise crosses his face. His brows lift as he stares at me, before saying flatly, "Sure. I need to take you in, anyway." He gestures impatiently, directing me to walk ahead of him.

Feeling my ire bubble a notch higher at his attitude, I stomp forward, hefting my soggy backpack over my shoulder with a huff.

Is it really too much to ask that when a hot guy finds a perfectly awesome girl, washed up on the beach, they be just a little bit amazed and enthralled? Really? I don't think that's a lot to ask. Little Mermaid ring any bells, mister?

Shooting a glare over my shoulder, I huff and puff my way up the beach, the man named Drake falling in mere steps behind me.

Grumpy, sodden, exhausted, silent tears well up and slip down my cheeks and I brush them aside. Sighing, I look up at the moonlit sky and mouth silently, *God... I'd really like a do-over of this day.*

Once we make it to the end of the beach, closer and closer to the lights, I slow down and fall behind Drake, following him. We have been silent the entire 10 minute walk, which is unnerving, but also a blessing, giving me time to think and figure out my next move.

I'm guessing my best bet is to attempt to talk to whomever is in charge on this island, and see if there is a way to get me back to the States. From there, I can just disappear into the seething mass of humanity that is Miami. Or wherever it is I wind up.

Panting still from the walk, covered in salt water and sand, I silently cheer when we reach a small community of what appears to be bungalows. *Thank you God! Hot shower, dry clothes, here I come.*

Trailing behind Drake, we make our way through the tiny community, people still out and about, enjoying the balmy night air. Staring around me, I notice everyone is dressed somewhat oddly.

My brow furrows. There are guards moving around the place, dressed like the man named Drake. Then there are even more people dressed in identical white or gray, robe-like garments. *Maybe you've stumbled onto an island monastery, Reagan.*

I smile inwardly, my sense of humor never failing to keep my spirits up, even when the world feels pretty grim indeed.

As we continue making our way to what looks to be a center bungalow in the middle of the community, obviously the hub of the place, the people in funny robes stop what they are doing and stare as we pass by. Feeling uncomfortable, I keep my head down, letting my hair hide my face as I trek behind Drake. *What, have these people never seen someone in normal clothes before?*

I let out a strangled laugh before I can stop myself, and Drake glances back my way, quirking a brow. I wave a hand, silently saying, *nothing, never mind. Just me, and the crazy catching up to me.*

I look up as we approach the center bungalow, and see three men standing there, also in robes. Albeit these robes are much fancier than what everyone else around here is wearing, pristine-looking and trimmed in gold designs. The one in the middle steps forward, holding out a hand.

"Greetings. We are the Elders of Halcyon Island. You can call me Elder Allen. And who might you be?"

Reaching out, I shake his hand gingerly. "Reagan. My name is Reagan. I, um... had a bit of a tumble off a cruise ship passing by your island, and wound up washed up on your beach." I jerk a thumb in Drake's direction. "Drake here, was kind enough to yank me out of the water and bring me to you." I recite my spiel as I'd been mentally rehearsing the last ten minutes, and then wait, trying not to hold my breath as the three Elders stare at me.

I stare back, lifting my chin a notch. Elder Allen looks to be quite old. 60's? 70's? Hard to tell with that head full of white hair. His eyes are narrow, and if I'm being 100% honest, somewhat creepy looking. Not sure why though. I shift uncomfortably. He hasn't given me any indication he's a creep, I just have spide-y vibes going wacky apparently.

The other two Elders step forward, introducing them-selves and offering their hands. "We are Elder James, and Elder John. Welcome to Halcyon Island." I shake both of their hands, but can't help noticing their expressions are sour. "You must be exhausted after your dip in the sea. And hungry. We can offer you some dry clothing and a meal, along with lodgings for the night, if you'd like."

I offer a polite smile, and my belly takes that moment to growl loudly. "Um... that would be great, thank you. I am pretty tired. Is there a boat I can hitch a ride on tomorrow, to take me back to the States?"

The two elders exchange a look, and begin talking in low voices between themselves. I shift on my feet, glancing at Drake before my gaze lands once again on Elder Allen. After his introduction, he's just been standing there, staring at me, with those creepy eyes. His stare isn't sexual or anything, not that I can tell, but still. I roll my shoulders back, straightening my spine and meeting his gaze squarely.

A tall man in a button down shirt and faded blue jeans walks up to our little group. *Wow. Someone NOT in a robe or a uniform.*

His sudden appearance interrupts what appears to be bickering between the two elders. They fall silent immediately, as soon as the man nears and opens his mouth. Stepping closer to me, he holds out his hand in welcome. I rub my palm down my wet, jean-clad thigh, then shake his obediently. *Geez, these people like to shake hands a lot.*

"Hey there. I'm David. I'm the leader of Halcyon Island." He smiles charmingly, and when he does, I notice his eyes crinkle at the corners. He is thin, sandy-haired, with a bit of grey just touching his temples. If I had to hazard a guess, I'd estimate him somewhere around the age of forty.

I smile back, less charmingly I'm sure, as I'm beginning to feel more than a little drained from my ordeal.

"Please, I know you must be tired. Elder Allen, I think that given the circumstances, this young woman should be allowed to stay the night, to rest from her ordeal. It's clear she has been delivered here by God Himself, and as His followers, we are to welcome her into our community with open arms, for as long as she might wish to stay." He looks pointedly at the other two elders, who clamp their lips shut, merely nodding.

Elder Allen nods too, his narrow eyes revealing nothing. "Agreed David. At least one night can do no harm, and we have already offered her such."

The man named David smiles again, offering me his arm with a small bow. "Please my dear, allow me to escort you to your lodgings for the night." I glance at Drake, who's been standing back and off to the side during all the introductions, and he just stares at me, his expression cryptic. *Okay, well, no loss there.*

I gingerly accept David's arm, allowing him along with a ragtag bunch of robed folks to lead me to the outskirts of the community, to a bungalow used for guests, or so I'm told.

As we walk, David takes that time to tell me more about the island of Halcyon.

"Halcyon my dear, in case you were wondering, is what we like to call a spiritual community. We are followers of God, and believe it's the divine right of everyone who steps foot on the island's shores, to stay here with us for as long as they feel called to stay. Our community is entirely self-sustained, with everyone here pulling their own weight and pitching in, to make it a place one is blessed to live in."

I nod, listening to the man go on about God, their spiritual way of life here on the island, and how they're all one big, happy family.

"But enough about us. I realize that on a strange island, surrounded by people you don't know, it may be a little uncomfortable for you to stay alone. So I've arranged for you to have a bit of company, if that suits you."

We stop in front of the small bungalow, and David motions with his hand. "Andie, step forward, please."

A young girl, wearing a long gray robe, steps out of the bunch that's been following us. She's got long, pretty, blonde hair, with wide eyes and a button nose. She looks to be about 16 as best I can tell, and more innocent than a toddler. She smiles at me warmly, her eyes sparkling with what looks like a mix of humor and eagerness. *Obviously these people get excited when strangers wash up on their shore.*

Holding out her hand, she says, "I'm Andie. Pleased to meet you." Squeezing her hand back, I mumble, "Reagan," and offer her a smile in return. I can't help but feel an instant sort of kinship with her, almost like she's a little sister. She's just that kind of soul, I suppose.

David speaks again, "Andie here, is one of Halcyon's most promising young people. I'm sure you will find her company comforting and refreshing during your stay here.

She also knows everything about the island and how things are done around here, so she will be a good resource for you, should you find yourself with questions."

Offering me another small bow, David motions for the rest of the crowd to follow behind him as he departs. "I'll leave you to rest for the night. Andie can provide you with clean dry clothing, and a meal for dinner. We can discuss your plans for your future in the morning, after breakfast."

"Thank you, David. I really appreciate the kind welcome and the place to stay. I'm sure Andie here will take great care of me." I look at Andie, and find her grinning. Unbidden, I grin back. I really can't help myself, her warmth just sort of radiates. With that, David and company take their leave, and Andie gestures for me to follow her inside the bungalow.

Rummaging around inside a tiny closet, Andie grumbles under her breath. I barely make out the words "I know there are extra jeans in here somewhere," and the rest just becomes gibberish.

Suddenly she gives a tiny shout of glee. "Aha! Found 'em." She turns to face me triumphantly, holding up a pair of jeans, a long-sleeved t-shirt, and some underwear.

She shoves the bundle of clothing into my arms, and then nods at a little screen off to the left of the small room.

"Bathroom is there. It's an open shower, but I'll make myself busy while you clean up, get the sheets changed and whatnot. This bungalow doesn't get used often."

Glancing in the direction she indicates, I nod. "Thanks. It would be nice to wash some of this salt and sand off before changing." I flash her a grateful smile.

She smiles back, her eyes full of sympathy. "There's soap and shampoo on the shelf. I have a brush too, I can run to my bungalow and grab it while you're showering." She pauses for a minute, and we both shift on our feet, staring at each other. "Okay, well, I'll leave you to it. Be back in a few."

With that, she's out the door, leaving me alone in the small wood framed room. I make my way to the showering area, carefully twisting the knob to turn the water on. Holding a hand under the spray, I wait for it to warm up before I begin peeling off my wet clothing. Grimacing at all the sand that falls off of me, I glance at the floor ruefully. Good thing this is an island. *They've got to be pretty used to sand everywhere, right?*

Jumping under the now hot spray, I quickly wash up, rinsing all of the beach and salt I can off of me, and using the soap to lather up my hair. *Definitely going to need that brush.*

Rinsing it out, I turn off the water and then stand for a moment, looking around the tiny space. Sighing in relief, I spot a towel folded neatly on a shelf, and make a grab for it. Wrapping it around myself, I flip my hair around, squeezing the water out and watching it spin down the now sandy drain.

I step out from behind the screen just as Andie enters the bungalow again, carrying a stack of sheets and blankets and pillows. She tosses me a brush, and I catch it instinctively.

Offering her a grin, I put the brush to work, untangling the knots from my hair as she speedily and efficiently makes the bed up, and creates a small cot for herself on the tiny couch off in the corner. Once I've got my hair sorted, I grab for the clothes and step behind the screen again to get dressed.

I tug a pair of jeans up my damp legs, surprised to find they fit almost perfectly. Makes sense, me and Andie look to be of similar size and build. Although, like Drake, and like quite a few of the new people I've met here for that matter, she's the yin to my yang when it comes to hair and features. Everyone around here seems to be blonde and tan.

Settling myself down onto the bed once it's made, I glance around the room. "So this isn't your bungalow? It's like a guest house?"

Andie nods. "Yes, my bungalow is across the community, on the other side. We could have stayed there for the night, but I wasn't sure if you'd feel comfy or not. I figured we can do the guest house tonight, and then if you end up staying awhile, I can show you my place and you can room with me." She smiles, her eyes warm and friendly. "I have an extra bunk in my bungalow, I used to share it with my older brother. But now that I'm 16, David thought it best that we share separate quarters, so I've been on my own for almost 6 months now. It'd be nice to have a roomie again."

I smile back at her. "Yeah, I can understand that. It's always nice to have company. Especially when you're used to living with someone for so long."

Andie nods. "Yeah, my brother has pretty much raised me since we were little kids, so it does feel a little weird, not having him in the same space as me. But David said it seems more appropriate, given our ages, to bunk by ourselves from now on." She shrugs. "What David says goes! Are you hungry at all?"

I put my hands on my belly, remembering I haven't eaten all day. "Yes, please. I'm starving!"

Andie grins. "I'll run grab you some food. It won't be much, maybe a sandwich or something. Is that all right?"

"Perfect!" I beam. "I could eat just about anything right now, I'm so hungry."

"Okay, I'll be back in a flash." With that, she's out the door again, the hinges squeaking gently as she goes. Scooting myself up to the head of the bed, I plump the pillows behind me, and curl my feet up. Putting my chin on my knees, I wait for her to return as I think about the events of the night, and the handsome but moody looking Drake who pulled me out of the water.

My lips twist. *Forget about the Drake guy, Reagan. He's obviously uptight and not interested in you one whit. Besides, you've got bigger things to worry about.*

I sigh, sitting up and scrubbing my hands through my damp hair. I almost can't believe I'm here right now. The day seems so surreal. I shake my head. I have no idea what I'm going to do once tomorrow comes, but I guess the only thing I can do right now is take it a day at a time. At least I'm not on Grandy Island. *Thank you God, for small favors.* I look up to the ceiling and grin, feeling quite pleased about that.

I jump a little when Andie breezes back into the room, carrying a small tray loaded down with a sandwich, a glass of milk, and a small bowl of fruit. My mouth waters just looking at it, and I hold out my hands eagerly.

"Thanks so much!" Settling the tray in my lap, I pick up the sandwich, biting into it with gusto. Andie perches on the side of the bed, watching me eat.

Mumbling around a mouthful of ~~food, I say~~, "So, tell me more about Halcyon. What's it like living here? It can't be easy on a young girl, alone. Do you ever feel scared or anything?"

Andie's eyes widen. "Oh no, I love it here! I honestly couldn't imagine living anywhere else. I've been here for as long as I can remember, so it's really just home for me. And everyone here is so amazing. I mean, we all love living here together, and everyone really cares for one another, y'know?

It's not like other places in the world, where everyone is just sort of out for themselves and stuff. We really take care of each other here."

Chewing my food and swallowing, I raise a brow, but nod agreeably. I can't help but feel a little skeptical. I mean, it'd be nice if a place like Andie describes exists, but the cynic in me can't help but question that.

Holding up my half-eaten sandwich, I mumble, "This is really good," and smile sheepishly. I keep my thoughts and doubts to myself however, at least for now.

IV

My eyes blink open slowly, as the light streaming in from the small window of the bungalow finally penetrates my surprisingly deep slumber. Stretching, I yawn, snuggling down deeper into the pillows and blankets I'm cuddled in, as the events of the day before stream back into my consciousness.

I hear a noise and lift my head to find Andie walking out from behind the small bathroom screen, braiding a headful of damp hair. She's still dressed in one of the funny robes, but I glimpse a jean-clad leg beneath when she moves. *So the robes must be some sort of uniform or something then.* She smiles brightly my way. "Oh good! You're awake! I was trying to be quiet, but it's almost time for breakfast. Are you hungry?"

My belly takes that moment to rumble again, so apparently I am. It's obvious my sandwich the night before didn't last long. I smile back at her, sitting up and pushing my hair out of my face, before croaking out, "Seems so." Clearing my throat, still thick with sleep, I grimace. Moving and sitting up reminds me of how many muscles I *don't* use enough. Every inch of my body feels sore and achy from my long swim the night before.

Andie looks concerned. "Are you all right? Are you in pain or something?"

Moving slowly, I lift a hand to calm her. "No, I'm good. Just a little sore from my swim last night." I smile ruefully. "Apparently I'm not in as great of shape as I'd thought."

Understanding dawns and Andie bobs her head. "Ahh, okay. Yeah, I imagine that was a pretty rough swim. The current can get real strong around the island, you're lucky you didn't end up in a riptide. Praise God you made it!" She smiles, then reaches for my hand, helping me up. "C'mon. I put an extra toothbrush in the bathroom. Freshen up, and we'll go eat."

"Yes m'am." I grin, then do as I'm told. My stomach does a little happy dance at the thought of a good breakfast, as I finish up and follow Andie out the door.

Andie and I make our way through the tiny community into the center, where there's a large, squat building simply called the Commons.

"Why's it called the Commons?" I ask, as we step through the doorway inside.

Andie shrugs. "I guess because it's sort of the common ground of the whole community here, where we all share life together. It serves multiple functions. We eat here of course," she gestures around at the tables and chairs set up neatly in rows, "and we have Worship services here. We also host all our community functions here too. Sort of the epicenter of our tiny island."

We make our way across the room to where the majority of people are congregated, forming a line. *Looks as though breakfast is buffet style. Yum.*

I push my hair behind my ear a little self-consciously as I notice many of the people staring at me. Glancing down at my jeans and tank top provided by Andie, my lips twitch. No doubt I stand out like a sore thumb considering I'm not clad in drapes like everyone else. My nose wrinkles as I scope out all the robes in the clear light of day. *Thank God for small favors. I'll stick with my jeans, thank you very much.*

Accepting a plate Andie hands to me, I step behind her in the line and move toward the buffet of food, my mouth already watering at all the smells. *Is that bacon? I loovve bacon.*

We shuffle forward, and begin piling food on our plates.

I try not to be greedy, but everything looks so good, I can't help but go a little overboard. Popping a grape in my mouth, I ask, "So, how did this place come to exist anyway? I mean, what started it? Who owns it? That David guy?"

Andie nods, popping a grape in her mouth too. I follow her through the line, and we make ourselves drinks to go with our plates of food.

"Yeah, David used to be a really popular evangelist in the States. Story goes, he had 'more money than God', and one day, God spoke to him and told him to gather up his most devoted followers, and take them on a pilgrimage to their new home. I've been here for as long as I can remember, but from what I've always been told, David invested everything he had into this island, into creating this community here."

"Wait, David is from the States? He was like one of those preachers or something you see on TV all the time?" Andie nods. "We don't have TV here, but yeah, from what I've been told, that's what he used to do."

"Huh. That's kind of crazy." I shake my head, feeling a little unsettled, but unable to put my finger on why.

"As the story goes, a lot of the older Halcyon members had very little to speak of, if anything at all, when it came to their former lives back in the States. They weren't like David, loaded or anything. In fact, he actually saved many of their lives by bringing them here with him, to Halcyon."

I frown, walking behind her a little more slowly as we

make our way to a table. The story sounds like a nice one, to be sure. I'm just not convinced that's all there is to it. My inner skeptic is nothing if not overly active.

Reaching the table, Andie stops, motioning for me to have a seat, next to two other people. "Reagan, this is Steps, and this is Robbie."

Both boys jump to their feet, the one called Robbie reaching to pull a chair out for me. "We already know who you are," Steps mumbles with a grin. "You're kinda famous around here. First person ever to wash up on our beach." Robbie elbows Steps and Steps shoots him a dirty look. "What? It's true."

Shaking his head Robbie sits back down, and Steps follows suit. Andie plops down in the chair next to me, popping another grape in her mouth. I sit too, offering both boys a smile of greeting, choosing to ignore references to my apparent fame.

Andie starts chitchatting with Steps while we all dig into our meals. Eyeballing the boys, I notice their plates are piled even higher than mine, so I feel marginally less gluttonous. Keeping quiet for the moment, I listen to the three of them chatter back and forth while we eat, studying all of them as I chew my food.

It's pretty obvious they're a tight little group. The one named Steps looks to be in his late 20's or so. Maybe a hair older than me. He's thin and rather nervous looking, with shaggy brown hair that keeps falling in his eyes, and he keeps jerking his head to clear them.

I look at Robbie. He's younger, more Andie's age I'd wager. He's pretty skinny too, but fit and strong, whereas Steps just looks skinny. His hair is dark, and he's sporting a pair of glasses, making him seem the bookish type. He's quiet, much more so than Andie or Steps, and appears focused, if a little hard to read.

Shoveling another big bite of scrambled eggs and hash into my mouth, I chew for a bit before speaking up, interrupting their chatter to ask, "So, why Steps?"

The three exchange looks, and Steps shrugs, grinning. "Well... lets just say I used to be a former addict of... ummm... certain illicit substances. I had to work the 12 steps program pretty often, but never quite managed to say clean. So, I was nicknamed Steps." He grins again. "I finally made it through the program and stayed clean the last time though, going on almost a year now. So I'm cool with the nickname. I think of it as a badge of honor, a testament to my desire to stay sober." He winks, then makes a little show of huffing on his nails and polishing them on his robe, prompting a smile from me at his humor.

I think it's awesome he's finally clean and made it through the entire program. I've known a lot of addicts in my short life, and it's never pretty.

"That's cool that you finally completed the program. Big achievement." Steps nods, his expression becoming more serious. "Yeah, I'd never have made it though, without this place. I'd be dead if it weren't for this island."

I nod. "So you like living here then." It's a statement more than a question. It seems that everyone I've met so far loves it here. I look to Robbie, "And you? What's your story?" Robbie just gives a little shake of his head, but doesn't offer much of an answer. "This place is home to me," he says simply. He doesn't add anything else, and I don't push him.

I take a sip of my water, nodding before glancing at my plate with an inward sigh. *Reagan, your eyes are definitely bigger than your stomach.* A rueful smile crosses my lips. I always seem to be ravenous, until I actually start eating. I grab my napkin, and start piling some of the left-overs into it, to take back to the bungalow and save for later, in case I get hungry between meals. It's mostly just grapes and some bread left anyway, so it should hold up for a few hours at least.

Andie looks over at me, her eyes widening. "Reagan! What are you *doing*?" I jump, startled by her loud exclamation, and meet her gaze. Her expression is horrified. Really? Horrified? Because I'm saving some food for later? My brows collide in confusion, and I glance at Robbie and Steps. Their faces are equally as horrified, although something in Steps' expression makes me question whether or not his is genuine.

"What? What did I do?"

Andie exchanges looks with Steps and Robbie, before

answering in a lower voice as she glances around the room, "We can't take food from the Commons. It's against the rules. We have mealtimes, and of course the Shepherds have rationed snacks at the Pen for when they are out in the heat all day, but that's it. David is very strict when it comes to stuff like that."

I put the food back on my plate, shocked. Careful not to show my feelings, I just nod. "Okay, sorry. No problem, I was just thinking it'd be great to have a snack later." I flash a wry smile and point to my stomach. "Always seems to be growling."

Andie and the two boys relax back into their chairs, chuckling and sharing relieved smiles. "Oh no problem, you didn't know, Reagan. You're new, so it will take some time for you to learn all the rules." Andie beams at me.

Seriously? People can't take food back to their bungalows here? I give a tight smile and a nod before glancing around the room. I notice Elder Allen, the man with the unnerving eyes from the night before, moving around the Commons from table to table, greeting community members as they eat.

I squirm in my chair, my stomach knotting. I don't know what it is about that man, but something just feels off. Andie notices my discomfort and gives me a reassuring smile.

"Don't worry, Reagan. Elder Allen can seem pretty intense sometimes, but he's alright."

Steps bristles. His response is subtle, but enough for me to pick up on, and I look his way curiously. "What-," my question is interrupted by the sight of Drake approaching our table.

My mouth snaps closed, and I can feel my face warming. *Lordy, blushing Reagan? Really?*

I shift in my chair again, annoyance mixed with attraction agitating me. Opening my mouth back up, I blurt out to the others, "Well, while you guys may have been impressed by my grand entrance on the beach, *that* one certainly was not." I jerk my chin in Drake's direction as he nears our table. "He acted more like he'd just found a rock in his boot or something." Steps snickers, and Robbie hides a smile.

Andie sits up straighter, clearing her throat and smiling at me apologetically, before motioning at the man called Drake. "Andie, meet Connor. My older brother."

I frown, confused. *I thought his name was Drake?*

Recovering quickly, I shake the stone-faced Connor's hand, saying, "I'm Reagan. Nice to meet you, Connor. Again." Unable to repress my curiosity, I ask, "So, Drake... is that your last name?"

Connor just looks at me, his expression unreadable. "Obviously," is his curt response. *His eyes are gray. Like thunderclouds.* The wayward thought distracts me from being offended at his rudeness, until Connor speaks again, looking at his sister. "You're supposed to take Reagan to see David," he mutters. He gives me another unreadable look and turns on his heel to stalk off. He doesn't seem particularly thrilled about that bit of news. I gape at his back, my annoyance ramping up a notch. It's coupled with bewilderment and my ever ready stubborn streak that is instinctively aroused.

So what, he doesn't want me talking to David or something? Is he afraid I might actually stay here? I close my mouth and lift my chin, sitting straighter, miffed. *Whatever.* Turning my attention back to the little group sitting around the table, I grumble, "What the heck is his problem anyway?" I look at Andie. She shrugs, exchanging looks with the other two boys.

"Connor is a Shepherd."

I frown. "A Shepherd?"

She nods, before explaining, "Everyone on the island, depending on their ages, have jobs. Or, as we prefer to label them, Callings. Being a Shepherd is Connor's Calling."

I must still look confused, because she continues, "Shepherds are a select number of community members who act sort of like guards over the Flock. The Flock being of course, the general members of the community. That's why he wears that uniform. All Shepherds are required to wear a uniform like Connor's at all times, when on duty."

Robbie nods, interjecting himself into the conversation. "That's probably what his problem is. He and the other Shepherds are wondering if you're a wolf or not. That's their job, to guard the Flock from wolves. Not literally of course. Figuratively."

Staring around the room as their words sink in, it hits me. This place looks quite a lot like a prison. Looking at the others, I say as much. Pointing at the uniformed guards and gesturing around the mess hall, I say, "This place isn't entirely unlike a prison, have any of you noticed?"

Andie lets out a tinkling laugh. "Oh, don't be silly. I mean, sure we have the guards and we all eat together and do things together and stuff. But we can leave at any time. Nothing at all like a prison." She smiles at me brightly, but I can't help noticing that Robbie and Steps remain silent, trading glances steeped in a story I'm not sure I want to be a part of.

V

After breakfast, I follow Andie to David's office. On the way, we pass children playing, and other people in robes, doing odd jobs here and there. Laundry, yard work, farming chores. Everyone seems very happy and friendly, nothing looks amiss. I still can't shake the tiny niggling of discomfort I feel though, like I'm missing something.

We reach David's office, and Andie knocks on the door, before giving me a smile and a wave. She walks off, and I stand there, waiting to be invited inside.

"Come in!" David calls. Stepping forward, I open the door cautiously, peeking my head around the edge. The first thing I notice is that the office is extremely modest. More like that of a head camp counselor than a leader of an entire community of people.

I step inside, and David motions me to take a seat in front of his desk while he finishes up an announcement over a push-button intercom on his desk about the day's activities.

When he's done, he smiles at me, his blue eyes fanning into little lines at the corners. "How did you fare through the night, Reagan? Are you enjoying your stay thus far? I hope you found breakfast suitable."

I nod, offering a small smile in return. "Yes, thank you. Everyone has been extremely kind and welcoming, and the food was delicious."

David nods, his eyes crinkling again. "So, what do you think of our humble little island community?" I'm not quite sure what he means, but I decide to be frank.

"Honestly, Halcyon and the community seems really great. Almost the 'too good to be true' kind of great. It's a little hard to believe a place like this even exists."

David's eyes lose some of the crinkle around them, and he studies me for a minute, before saying, "Well, if you put a little trust and faith in people, more often than not, they will surprise you."

I snort. "Right." *That's what got me arrested in the first place. Trusting people.*

Almost as though he's reading my mind, David changes the subject. "Well, I imagine the nearest cruise route that I know of would have been quite the swim," he offers a little pointedly. I can feel my cheeks heat, and keep my gaze centered on his desk. *Point taken, buddy.*

It's true that I'm not being exactly honest with the people of Halcyon, but I have good reason. So I merely shrug, and say mildly, "People manage to do incredible things when faced with the possibility of death."

David nods, lacing his fingers together on top of his desk. "Indeed, that they do." Then he gives me a direct look. "Reagan, I'm sure you know that you are welcome to stay or go as you please, no matter your situation elsewhere in the world. But perhaps you should just be straight with me, and tell me the truth of your plight, so that I can help you figure out what to do next."

His eyes feather at the corners again, and he smiles at me disarmingly. Against my better judgment, I find myself softening, wanting to open up to him. I wriggle in my chair, looking out his office window, while he sits patiently, waiting for me to speak.

Sighing, I mentally shrug, before spilling the beans on my entire story. "I had a friend, back in Miami. Her name was Claire, and she sort of fell in with a bad crowd. At first it was pretty harmless, some light drug use, but it soon escalated to harder stuff." I pause, swallowing, my mouth feeling dry all of a sudden.

David smiles encouragingly. "Would you like some water?"

I nod, and he gets up to grab a small bottle of water from

a tiny fridge behind his desk. I accept the offering with gratitude, taking a long gulp to soothe my unexpectedly parched throat.

Taking one last swig, I put the cap back on before continuing, "One night, I got a call from Claire. She was in some seedy hotel room, holed up with some guy who took a turn into crazy. She said he was wired out of his mind, ranting and raving, and begged me to come and get her."

I scrub a hand through my hair, thinking back to the night that landed me in this mess. "I don't like getting involved in that sort of stuff, but Claire was my friend. I couldn't just leave her stuck in a situation like that."

David nods, only commenting with, "That's understandable."

I keep going, "I arrived at the seedy hotel just in time apparently. Captain Cokehaze was in a rage, trashing the room, and Claire was cowering in the bathroom, hiding, about to pass out because she was coming down hard."

"I heard someone outside yelling about the police coming, and I hurry, trying to get Claire out of there with as little fuss as possible. Claire mumbled something about her bag, and I saw it on the bathroom floor, and made a grab for it. Didn't think anything of it at the time. Then I half-carried her outside, trying to drag her out of there as quickly as I could, doing my best to get us both anywhere but there."

I swallow hard, feeling the fear I felt then, and the anger

too. "Before we could make it very far, we were surrounded by police, who apparently had been called because of a noise complaint. Probably because of Captain Cokehead and his crazy." I roll my eyes. "Little did I know, Claire's bag was full of his cocaine, and that's why the dude was so psycho. Claire stole it from him, and he'd been looking for it, which was what put him into a rage and resulted in the noise complaint."

"I wound up stuck in an impossible situation. We were hauled in and booked, and Claire, the little weasel, pled out for a lesser charge in exchange for selling me out for my supposed 'drug dealing.'" My eyes well with tears as I remember the sense of betrayal and fury I'd felt when I found that out. I blink them back, and firm my lips, meeting David's gaze. "Needless to say, Claire skated by with nothing more than probation, and I was sentenced to a stint at the Grandy Island Reintegration Facility. And *that*, is how I wound up *here*."

Wringing my fingers together, I drop my gaze to my lap as I wrap up my tale of woe. I can feel David studying me, and I fidget some more. *Geez, say something already.*

Looking up through the fringe of my lashes, I see David lean back in his chair, folding his arms across his chest. Finally, he speaks, "Reagan, I don't believe you are here by accident. I believe God saw your travails, saw the injustice that was done to you, and that He had a different plan for you altogether. I believe His plan was to bring you here, to stay here with us, which is certainly more appealing than your alternatives, I would imagine. Going through the rest of life as a fugitive, with the possibility of getting caught and handed an even harsher sentence is certainly no way to live."

He pauses, as though weighing his words. "The way I see it, Reagan, you have two options. You can leave immediately, we can arrange for a boat to take you back to the States and deposit you somewhere inconspicuous. Or you can remain here, indefinitely. You can make friends, contribute to the community, and of course, should you one day decide you want to leave, you are perfectly able to do so."

Lifting my gaze, I meet David's. His eyes are still crinkled at the corners, like he's perpetually happy, and his expression though not unkind, gives away nothing. Still, trusting someone just doesn't come naturally for me. I decide to put him to the test.

"If those are my options, David, I'd like to leave," I state formally, with a stiff incline of my head. He only smiles, then picks up a radio and tells someone on the other end to prepare The Ark. My eyes widen, and he chuckles. "Just messing with you, Reagan." He speaks into the radio again, "Scratch that, prepare a boat please."

Slumping back into my chair, I hesitate. He does seem perfectly willing to let me leave. I chew my bottom lip as he continues speaking into the radio to someone, before blurting out, "Wait!"

He looks back at me, finger on the radio button, and raises a brow.

"I've changed my mind... I'd like to stay."

David smiles broadly, prompting me to smile back, albeit cautiously. "As you wish."

After making another call into his radio, Andie arrives again.

"Andie, please take Reagan on a tour of the community of Halcyon, so she can decide if any of the various Callings seem like something she might want to do with her time here. It's important for her to find her place, so that she feels at home. Also, since you have a spare bunk in your bungalow anyway due to your recent split from your brother, I'm assigning Reagan to live with you."

Andie nods, beaming, practically vibrating with excitement over learning I plan to stay and will be rooming with her like she'd hoped. "Yes, sir." She grins, grabbing my hand and tugging me from David's office. "C'mon, let's go!"

VI

Andie all but drags me through the community, talking excitedly, pointing out the various jobs and duties the people of Halcyon share.

"There's laundry, farming, childcare, the medical clinic, even a small theater charged with community entertainment. A handful of members specialize in putting on plays, puppet shows, and stand-up comedy, all family-friendly of course."

I watch as a Shepherd talks to a couple of kids, before I interrupt Andie's stream of words. "I've made up my mind." She stops talking, looking over at me in surprise. "You have?"

I nod, and point with my chin. "I want to be a Shepherd."

Andie's mouth forms a tiny 'O', her brow furrowing,

before she nods. "Okay. If that's what you think you're feeling called to do. David will have to approve it of course."

I nod, my lips curving upward in a smile. "Of course."

The big decision made, Andie grabs my hand again. "C'mon. Let me show you my... *our*... bungalow." She hauls me along behind her once more and we make our way across the community to a little bungalow with cheerful flowers next to the door.

Stepping inside, I look around. I can't help but smile, because the place is so clearly Andie. Cheerful, with the windows thrown wide to let in the light, and girly curtains blowing in the breeze. There's a small brightly colored rug in the center of the floor, and two bunk beds pushed up against one wall, both covered in matching quilts.

Andie grins, spinning around to look at me. "You can have the top bunk." Then she lets out a strangled squeal, grabbing me up in a tight hug. "This is going to be so much fun! It's like having a sister move in with me!"

I hug her back, offering her a smile of my own. I can't shake the tiny shiver of misgiving that washes through me, but do my best not to let it show on my face.

Besides, it kind of *will* be like living with a sister. I haven't known Andie long, but that's exactly what she feels like to me, a younger sister. Already I can tell I'm becoming attached, and I can only pray this situation works out. *Please God, let all of this work out.*

After Andie showed me to our shared housing, and we'd made the rounds of the compound checking everything out, I wind up back at our bungalow for a much-needed nap. Things have been moving so quickly I'm not sure my body and brain have quite caught up. Andie offered to make herself scarce so that I could sleep uninterrupted, and I took her up on it with gratitude.

After climbing onto my bunk, I sigh, wiggling to get comfortable. Before I know it, I must have fallen asleep because it seems I'd no sooner closed my eyes than I hear a knock at the door, and I blink them open. I note the long shadows in the room coming from the windows and realize the sun must be setting.

Lying there another minute, trying to get my bearings, I hear a second tap. *The door. Someone's at the door.*

Shaking off the dregs of sleep, I sit up, swinging my legs over the side of the bunk and dropping to the ground. Making my way to the door, I open it just as another tap begins. I squint, bleary-eyed, the setting sun blinding me for a second to someone standing in front of me. He's just a shadow, the sunlight blazing around him like a halo, so it takes me a moment to realize it's David.

"Oh, hello David. I'm sorry, I was just taking a nap. I must have been more tired than I thought."

I take a step back, opening the door wider and inviting him inside. He smiles, dipping his head and entering the room. I'm just about to shut the door when he speaks.

"Leave it open please. Propriety you know. Just prop it with the little door stop there."

I raise my brows as I turn away to do as he asks, opening the door wider and placing the stop in front of it. The waning sunlight streams into the little room, warming the floor and giving everything a cheerful glow.

Turning back to face David, I offer him a tentative smile of my own. "So what brings you by?"

His brow furrows, and he begins wandering around the room, his tall frame filling up the space surprisingly well. "Ah yes. My purpose. Andie tells me you've made the rounds of the compound and have decided you'd like to be a Shepherd. Is this accurate?"

I frown. *Why wouldn't it be?*

Instead of saying that, I only nod the affirmative. "Yes, that's accurate. I think the Shepherd role would suit me well."

David studies me, wagging his head up and down thoughtfully. "I see. I would like to remind you that the role of Shepherd is quite a special role here in our community. It's not one to be taken on lightly. Are you certain there isn't some other area you feel you'd be better suited for, Reagan?"

My skin does a little crawling thing at the way he says my name, but I can't for the life of me figure out why. He seems nice enough. He's very polite and charismatic. Quite charming actually, to others at any rate. But just the way he says my name sends a warning tingle along my spine, and I can't get rid of it.

I shake my head instead. "No, I think the role of Shepherd will suit me just fine. You've stated that our participation in the community is supposed to be our 'Calling', right?"

David nods his head. "Yes, yes, that's true."

"Well if that's the case, I'd remind you to consider the story I shared with you earlier today, about my friend Claire. She was lost, and in need of guidance and direction. I was there to help her to the best of my abilities, which I understand is part of the role of a good Shepherd. Doesn't that sound then, like being a Shepherd would be my Calling?"

I face him squarely, meeting his charismatic blue gaze with my own dark one. His eyes crinkle at the corners once more, like he's ever ready to smile, yet he doesn't.

Dropping his gaze, he paces around the room with slow steps, clearly mulling over my response and giving what I just said some deep thought. His arms are crossed, and he taps his chin and stares at the floor as he walks. Finally, he speaks, "You make a very valid point Reagan. It does indeed sound as though being a Shepherd could be your true Calling."

He spins on his heel to face me once more, giving a brisk nod. "I'm willing to allow it. On a trial basis of course. My goal is to make sure all members of the flock are assigned where they are truly gifted and meant to be assigned, and if I find that any role taken on doesn't seem to be a good fit, then it's time to reassess. So let's agree to a two week trial as a Shepherd, and see how things go. Sound suitable?" He lifts a brow, giving me a questioning look.

I swallow and nod my head in agreement. "Yes, sure... I'm good with that." *Reagan... what are you getting yourself into?*

VII

The next morning, Andie is up and gone when I wake up. Getting dressed in the clean clothes she'd thoughtfully left lying out for me, I scrub my teeth and tie back my hair, before making my way to the door to go looking for people.

When I open it and step outside, I'm greeted almost immediately by the man called Elder Allen. He walks up to me with a reluctant wave hello.

I wave back and wait for him to get closer. "Hi Reagan, good morning. I don't know if David told you, but I'm Overseer of the Shepherds. I'm here to show you to Shepherd's Pen and get you started." He doesn't sound particularly pleased with his assignment.

"Oh okay. I was wondering where to go this morning, thank you," is all I offer in response.

Elder Allen folds into a small half bow, and then extends his arm, pointing the way. "Please, follow me." I do as he says, following behind him and observing the hustle and bustle of morning life on the compound. People are already out and about, starting their duties for the day. Some kids are laughing and shouting. One older lady is beating out a rug as we pass by, and offers me a toothy grin. I grin back, unable to resist.

We walk, winding our way through the compound. Along the way, Elder Allen shares a bit about himself. "I've been a Shepherd ever since I came to this island. Quite a long time ago, in fact. Being a Shepherd is a big responsibility young lady, it's been my whole life's focus. I truly hope you're prepared for it." I bristle at his condescending tone but don't bother engaging. It's obvious the man isn't thrilled with my choice of a Calling.

He continues, "It's my... *our*... job to oversee the Flock and protect them from all threats, both internal and external. That is our only purpose as Shepherd. Being Overseer here, it's also my job to lead all of you, and teach you what it means to be a good Shepherd. I truly pray that you will be an asset to this mission, and that you will not disappoint me." He glances behind him, looking my way.

Once more, I bristle at his tone, but ignore it. "I will

do my best, Elder Allen." I keep my back straight and my shoulders stiff, staring ahead as we walk, not giving him the courtesy of my gaze. I sneer once his back is to me again. *Crotchety old man.*

We walk for several minutes more in silence before approaching a small, squat bungalow.

Elder Allen waves a hand in the direction of the structure, stating, "This is Shepherd's Pen. That's what we call it, but you might also call it headquarters. It's where all the Shepherds get organized for the day's work. You can shower here if needed, and there are always snacks and drinks on hand."

Before he finishes his sentence, Connor emerges through the front door, walking out to greet us. He's scowling, and it's clear he's another one who isn't thrilled by my choice of a Calling. At least Elder Allen is relatively polite about it though. Connor is just downright rude. *And scowl-y.*

I offer him a small wave hello, as he and Elder Allen speak to each other quietly off to the side. I can hear Elder Allen telling Connor to show me the ropes and get me a uniform. Everything else is too low for my ears to catch. Connor just keeps scowling and nodding before finally glancing over at me.

Elder Allen gives me a wave, saying, "I'm leaving you with Connor now. If you have any questions or need any help, he's your guy." He looks pleased to be shunting me off to someone else, if his expression is any indication.

Connor just stands there, hands dangling down by his sides, staring at me for a few minutes before barking, "C'mon. I'll show you the Pen and get you a uniform."

He spins on his heel and starts stalking to the front door. It's clear that's all I'm getting from him, so I give a mental shrug and follow behind him as he heads into the building.

Inside, the structure is clean and tidy, and bigger than its outside appearance leads one to believe. I follow Connor to a small room with the label Showers above the door, and he steps inside. I follow him, somewhat cautious as I look around. It's sort of like a locker room, with benches, showers, toilets, and a shelf with cubbies.

Opening a closet door, he rummages around, yanking out two uniforms. He shoves them at me, and I catch them, holding them to my chest. Funny enough, the female versions are identical to the male versions. Guess they don't really expect many females to be Shepherds. I give a silent groan. *Chauvinistic much?*

"You can change in there." He points at some small stalls with curtains that hang around them. "When you're done, come out that door and hang a left to the main room. I'll introduce you around." He moves as if to leave, getting all the way to the door, before stopping, and turning around to face me. He looks as though he wants to say something, and I lift a brow, staring at him. He opens and closes his mouth, then scrubs a hand over his face before pinning me with eyes darker than my own. *Beautiful eyes.*

I stomp the wayward thought down, and continue to stare at him with a questioning look. "Welcome to the Shepherds," he mutters, before spinning on his heel and slamming his hands against the door, throwing it wide open and letting it swing shut with a thump behind him.

I just stand there, frowning and staring at the space he occupied for a few minutes, before heading to a stall to get changed. *Geez. What is that guy's problem?*

I feel a little self-conscious in my Shepherd's uniform. It fits more snugly than I thought it would, and while I'm not voluptuous by any stretch, the uniform does a great job of clinging to what little curves I have, making me appear more feminine than I'm comfortable with. You'd think the uniform would have had the opposite effect, given that it's designed more for men. I grimace, throwing my things in one of the cubbies once I'm changed and making my way out the door, in search of the main room.

It's not difficult to find -- the building isn't very large.

The main room is occupied by a handful of workstations equipped with desks, and not a whole lot else. Sitting at one of the desks is a woman with a ponytail. At least I'm fairly certain she's a woman. *Good to know they aren't as chauvinistic as I thought then. Seems they just don't like me in particular.*

To be fair, she looks like she fits right in as one of the guys. She's extremely toned and strong looking, with tanned skin, and a sharply angled face. She appears competent and capable. I imagine if we were to be embroiled in a bar fight or some such situation, she'd be the only one to walk away unscathed. She just seems to be that sort. I gulp, feeling disconcerted. Even more so when she catches sight of me and leaps to her feet, making her way over. I notice her eyes are a murky colored green, but pretty and thickly lashed.

She strides toward me, her gait purposeful, and reaches out to pump my hand up and down enthusiastically. "You must be Reagan! Welcome! So glad to have you on board." I offer a weak smile, inwardly wincing at the strength of her grip. *Owww...*

I gently disengage my fingers as Connor walks up. "Reagan, meet Laney. Laney, this is Reagan. As you already seem to know." His tone is dour, almost as dour as his expression. I shoot him a grumpy look of my own, getting tired of being the target of his bad attitude, then smile at Laney. "Hey Laney, nice to meet you. Thanks for the warm welcome." I give Connor a pointed glare, and he only rolls his eyes. *Gah. The nerve of the man.*

I'm distracted by the approach of another male, this one black, looking to be in his late 20's or so. He's also quite buff, looks to be the type who can definitely handle his own. *Sheesh. What's everyone do around here, pump iron in their downtime?*

He grins broadly as he gets closer, even, white teeth shining out from his dark face like a beacon of light, changing his whole demeanor from formidable to kind of sweet. I grin back in response, unable to help myself.

He holds out a hand, his forearm muscled and striped with rope-like veins. I eye his hand warily, remembering Laney's grip, before allowing him to take my hand in his own. His grasp is surprisingly gentle. "Hey there. I'm Terrence." He gives my fingers a squeeze before letting them go.

I let exhale a tiny breath of relief before replying, "I'm Reagan. Which I guess you also already know." My lips quirk and my glance travels back to Connor, who looks equal parts bored and impatient.

Terrence only nods, glancing at Connor as well before giving him an elbow in the ribs coupled with a glower. Connor grunts, the wind whooshing from his lungs before glaring at Terrence. "Hey... what was that for?"

Terrence and Laney both ignore him, refocusing their attention on me. Laney speaks, "You'll have to forgive

Connor his manners. It's not you personally, it's just Connor being Connor. He can be a jerk sometimes, unintentionally of course." I sneak a peek at Connor's face. *Nope. I'm pretty sure it's intentional.*

Once again, I resist an urge to stick my tongue out at him like a 4 year old. Terrence cuts in, saying, "Yeah, he doesn't mean to be a dunce. It's just his nature." He chuckles, before continuing, "Really though, it's just that we all take being a Shepherd seriously. Connor here, he just forgets to breathe sometimes." Terrence gives Connor another elbow in the ribs, and this time Connor grunts and grimaces, but doesn't say anything, only shooting Terrence another mutinous glare. Laney has a teasing grin on her face, so it's clear that these two enjoy ribbing Connor about his dour attitude. I hide a smile, liking them both already.

I look at Connor, meeting his gaze. "So, are you in charge here then? Elder Allen directed you to show me around, so I assume you are."

He shakes his head no. "Shepherds have no rank below Elder Allen. He's our leader, and we're all just Shepherds. We do what Shepherds do, no one is above or below anyone else." His tone is grudging, like he doesn't really want to answer my question but feels he has no choice.

He stands up straighter, giving Laney and Terrence pointed looks. "You two chumps ready to patrol, show Reagan how things work around here?" They both look at each other and grin, sharing an inside joke before nodding in agreement and speaking in unison. "Sure, we're ready."

I hide another smile, experiencing a strange inner glee at their ribbing and poking fun of Connor. He seems like he needs a reminder once in a while that life isn't as grim as he seems to think.

Keeping silent, I follow the three of them out the door of the bungalow, stepping out into the bright sunlight and blinking as my eyes adjust. *Time to see what being a Shepherd is all about.*

VIII

I trail Connor, Terrence, and Laney all around the compound, mostly observing. Along the way, we stop and talk to several members of the community, just making conversation, commenting on the weather, the wife, this and that. It all feels very routine and mundane, nothing extraordinary or out of the norm.

When we have a break in between conversations with the Flock, I ask, "Do any of the Shepherds carry firearms or anything? Are firearms even allowed on the island?"

They all exchange glances and then Connor responds, "We have the tools and means to protect ourselves if necessary, but in the entire history of the island, there's never been a reason for a Shepherd or anyone else to use, or even carry firearms."

Huh. That seems almost too ideal to be truth.

My train of thought is interrupted when Connor stops walking, and I almost run into the back of him. Peering around his shoulder, Laney and Terrence flanking me, I see Steps wandering around near some trees at the edge of the area designated for farming, as best I can tell.

Connor looks over his shoulder at me, his gaze intent, before heading in Steps' direction. Not sure what's going on, I follow him, listening as he confronts Steps when we get within talking distance.

"Hey, Steps, what are you doing out here?" Connor's tone is tinged with suspicion and I watch them both with curiosity. "This isn't your area. Your Calling is over in the Workshop, where the entertainers practice."

Steps has a look on his face that I can only assume is guilt, mixed with a healthy dose of chagrin. He glances at me, and I frown. Terrence and Laney move past me, fanning out and checking out the nearby woods. I look over at Connor. "Why does it matter what Steps is doing out here?"

He shoots me an impatient glare. "Part of our job is to make sure all members of the Flock are where they are supposed to be, doing what they have been Called to do. This is how all members are kept safe."

Glancing around us again, our surroundings appear benign and harmless. Brow furrowing deeper, I wonder out loud, "Kept safe from what?"

Terrence overhears me as he gets closer, having found nothing of importance during his search, and answers, "In Steps' case, it could be almost anything."

He and I exchange glances, leaving me still confused. I look to the woods when Laney gives a little shout, indicating she's found something. Grabbing the item, she starts loping our way, her stride strong and swift, even at the slower pace.

Holding it up, she crows, "It's a sack. Full of food it looks like, I found it buried beneath a bush." Steps' face turns a faint crimson color, and he doesn't look happy.

Connor claps Steps on the shoulder, gripping him and pushing him into motion. "You know I'll need to notify Elder Allen of this, man." Steps remains silent, his jaw set, and doesn't bother to respond. Connor shakes his head, rolling his eyes to the sky, giving Steps another small shove. "C'mon. Let's get to the Pen."

We all fall in line behind Connor and Steps, pacing behind them silently for several minutes as we make our way back to Shepherd's Pen.

Finally, unable to keep my mouth shut or my thoughts to myself, I blurt, "I don't understand. Why does it matter if Steps is hoarding food in the woods? I don't get it. Andie said I couldn't take any food back to my bungalow after breakfast either. What's the harm in stashing a little food away?" *Granted, hiding it in the woods seems a little weird, but to each their own I guess.*

Connor doesn't slow down to respond. Talking over his shoulder, he tells me, "Hiding food out in the woods can be a sign of any number of things, all of which are frowned on by our community. He could be running a gambling ring somewhere, or be involved in some kind of black market operation, or even just hiding and eating the food himself. In which case, that counts as gluttony. That's why Andie stopped you from taking food back to your bungalow. We don't do gluttony here." His tone is flat, and he shoots me a glower over his shoulder before facing forward again, stalking behind Steps.

Frowning, I stare at Connor's back, mulling over his words, never mind his crappy attitude.

Laney touches my arm gently, and I look over at her, startled from my thoughts. She smiles. "Speaking of food, would you like to eat dinner with us tonight? Connor, Terrence, and I?"

Before I can respond, I overhear Connor mumbling something under his breath. I can't make out the words, but I feel my face warm with embarrassment and irritation. *OK buddy, I get it. You don't like me. Get over it.*

Laney gives me a little nudge as we walk, though it doesn't feel very little. The woman doesn't seem to know her own strength. "Ignore grumpy up there. He's just being a sourpuss. We won't hear of you eating anywhere else. You're a Shepherd now. We stick together."

Offering her a tight smile in response, I nod my head, still glaring at Connor's well-muscled back.

Apparently he didn't get the memo.

I sniff, lifting my chin as I continue to follow the small group to the Pen.

At dinner, I sit with my newfound friends and partners, listening to their chatter back and forth as I eat my food. I'm hungrier than I realized -- the day has been long and hot.

Once my food is gone, I break into the conversation, asking Connor something that's been buzzing in the back of my mind ever since the whole Steps incident.

"Connor, do you really think this is the right sort of place for your little sister to grow up?"

Everyone at the table falls silent, looking to Connor. I squirm in my seat, but don't retract my question, and meet his gaze squarely.

Connor takes another bite of food, before replying in an annoyed tone, as though speaking to someone slow, "Andie is safe here, Reagan. She has structure, and friends, food and clothing, a roof over her head. She has everything here she could possibly need."

My brows collide, anger sparking inside me at his condescending response. "Umm, if Andie were to *possibly* need some snacks between meals, she wouldn't have that, now would she?" I snap.

Connor's expression darkens, his gaze meeting mine. I cringe inwardly, already regretting my sharp tongue, though I'm not sorry for stating the truth, even if it's not my place. He stands abruptly, shoving his chair out behind him, and stalks off without another word, leaving his meal half-eaten on the table.

I stare after him, my mouth falling open. Laney lets out a nervous chuckle, grabbing my attention. "Don't worry, Reagan. Connor will get over it. He always gets intense when it comes to anything regarding his sister." She gives me an encouraging smile, while Terrence wags his head up and down next to her in agreement. I have to smile, they are always so in sync. I wonder if they're dating or something, but it's been hard to tell... they don't show any obvious displays of affection that I've noticed.

Laney continues, "Connor has raised Andie pretty much all on his own since they were kids, and he can't imagine he would have been able to do that all these years without this place as his support system." Her tone is admiring, and she's looking at the door Connor disappeared through with fondness.

I stare at the door thoughtfully. Maybe I've been too quick to judge him. It's obvious Laney and Terrence both seem to like and respect Connor, and Laney appears to admire his connection and devotion to his sister. *Could I be wrong about him?*

I shift uncomfortably, not liking the direction of my thoughts. I'm usually a good judge of character, but ever since Connor found me washed up on the beach, something about him just gets under my skin, riling me up.

Deciding a change of subject is in order, I look over at Terrence. "So, what's your story? Laney tells me she was born here, but how about you?"

Terrence and Laney exchange looks, with Terrence appearing less than comfortable at the change in topic. His expression turns sad and he replies, "I made some crappy choices as a kid. We were born poor, and I got caught up in gang life in my old neighborhood. My mom got shot by a bullet meant for me when I was 14, and that's around the time I met David. He offered me a new life and a new start, and I took him up on it... me and Laney here have been Shepherding together ever since."

Laney reaches over and gives Terrence's hand a squeeze. "And we both know God works in mysterious ways. Even though the circumstances are sad, we would never have met otherwise." She smiles at me, and I realize my suspicions are confirmed as I look at their clasped fingers.

I smile back, and reach over to give Terrence an awkward pat on the shoulder. "I'm sorry to hear about your mom, but I imagine Laney is right. I'm beginning to realize there's always a purpose for things, if we take the time to look hard enough and find it."

We all sit and chat for a while longer, finishing up the last of our meals, when I notice Andie across the room at another table. It also occurs to me that I haven't seen Steps since we arrived for dinner. I offer Terrence and Laney a quick smile before excusing myself, leaving them alone to go talk to Andie. If anyone might know something, I'm certain it'd be her.

IX

Winding my way through the room, members of the Flock talking and laughing as I pass by them, I reach the table I spotted Andie at, talking to Robbie.

Andie looks up at me and flashes one of her megawatt smiles. "Hey Reagan! How'd your first day as a Shepherd go? I hope my brother wasn't too rude."

Sitting down in an empty chair next to her, I lean over and whisper into her ear, "Do you know where Steps is?"

Andie leans back and looks at me, her expression confused. "Steps? Why would I know anything about where Steps is?" She glances at Robbie and he just shrugs, indicating he's lost too.

I sigh. Obviously the two of them don't know anything about today's earlier events. Sitting up straighter, I start talking. "I was out on patrol today with Connor, Terrence, and Laney. We got out near the woods by the farmlands, and saw Steps lurking about. Long story short, Laney found a sack of food hidden in the woods, and we confiscated it and took Steps back to the Pen. Then I changed and got ready for dinner, and I haven't seen him since."

I cross my arms, looking at the two of them, lifting a brow. Andie laughs lightly, trading looks with Robbie. He laughs too, although his seems more forced. Andie comments, "You know, I love Steps, but that boy has problems. This place is exactly the right kind of environment for him, he needs the structure." She shakes her head, stirring her food around on her plate. "He's probably in counseling or something with Elder Allen. Nothing to worry about, that's what usually happens when someone is caught bending community rules. It's not fun, but nothing to be alarmed about either." She looks up and offers me an encouraging smile. "I'm sure that must be where he is, and he's doing just fine."

Robbie doesn't say anything, but nods his head in agreement when I look over at him.

I sigh and lean back in my chair, staring around the room as Robbie and Andie resume their conversation. My eyes move restlessly over the small sea of faces, some of them familiar now, others not so much. But no Steps.

Still feeling as though something isn't right, I decide that as a Shepherd, it's perfectly within my rights to be concerned and to look into the matter more deeply. Maybe I need to take my worries to one of the other Shepherds. Decision made, I excuse myself once again, making my way to the door of the building. I'll just head over to the Pen and speak with someone. I'm sure if I voice my concerns, they will look into it.

They have to, right? *I hope.*

Nightfall has started to settle over the island, with stars emerging to twinkle in the sky, and a bright full moon beginning to make its ascent. I breathe in the warm, balmy air as I step outside. I love the smell of beach and salt water. You'd think I would love it a little less after my harrowing dip in the sea, but if anything I love it even more now. *Appreciation for survival and all that.*

I wander my way slowly to Shepherd's Pen, enjoying the quiet night and the peaceful walk. My worries over Steps almost melt away. *Almost.*

Then I see the lights of the Pen looming in the distance and they all come flooding back. I've begun to really worry about Steps and what may have happened to him over his minor "transgression". *Hiding a sack of food of all things.* I snort, the sound loud in the relative quiet.

Reaching the Pen, I roam through the building, looking for some of the other Shepherds. My search is fruitless though, there's no one here, despite the lights blazing. Shaking my head, I stop and stand for a few minutes, just staring around the room. *Why isn't anyone here if the lights are all on?*

I shrug my shoulders, and decide to head back to my bungalow and get some sleep. It's clear I'm not going to find anyone to help me tonight. Heading out the door, I flip off the lights to the Pen as I go, and then stop, my eyes caught by something. Squinting, I stare at the floor near the wall and realize I'm seeing light streaming up through the floorboards. My brow furrows.

The Pen has a basement?

I step closer, hearing noises but unable to make out what they are. My frown deepening, I quietly look around the Pen, trying to find a door that I know doesn't belong to a closet or lead outside. Spotting what I'm looking for, I stride across the room, careful to move as silently as I can.

Opening the door slowly, I stare down a set of stairs, my heart starting to pound. Light streams upward, illuminating the stone wall and wooden railing lining down the stairwell. Holding my breath, I listen and hear the noises again. Sharp cracking sounds, followed by what sounds like whimpering.

I tiptoe down the stairs, my heart lurching unsteadily in my chest. I grip the wooden railing with my fingers in a death grip as I go, fear and anxiety over what I'm about to find rippling through me. I almost reach the bottom when Elder Allen appears in my line of sight, and I stumble at the last step. A gasp escapes my lips when I see what's happening, and I almost fall, barely catching myself before I do.

Steps is bound, tied tightly to some sort of wooden structure, and Elder Allen is savagely whipping him with a cracked leather belt. I put a fist to my mouth, biting down on a cry of distress, eyes widening at the sight of poor Steps' back, welted and marked by the vicious blows.

Elder Allen spins around when he hears me, breathing hard, his eyes glinting in the light. When he sees me, he chuckles, running the belt through his fingers. "Hey there Reagan." He holds the belt out in my direction. "Want a turn?"

My eyes flash to the belt, to Steps tied and quivering, to Elder Allen's smirking face. I feel bile rise in my throat and I start to back up the stairs. Feeling sick to my stomach, I spin on my feet and dart up the steps, sprinting across the room and bursting through the doorway outside, into the open night air. I keep running, putting as much distance between myself and the Pen as I can before stopping, bending over and sucking in heaving breaths. I'm shivering, and a cold sweat has broken along my brow. *What the hell is going on in this place?*

Standing up straight, I put my hands against my sides

and walk around in small circles, trying to calm myself and cool down from my unexpected sprint. I breathe in slow, deep breaths, my mind racing.

I have no idea what to do. I'm not sure going to Andie is the best move. I don't know if she'll just blow me off. I'm not even sure if she's capable of accepting what I have to tell her. She's so attached to this place. There's no one else on this island that I come close to trusting more than Andie. I feel torn and alone, and cross my arms, rubbing them briskly as gooseflesh breaks out in a sudden attack of chills.

Does David know what's going on here? What Elder Allen is doing right now, to Steps? Or is Elder Allen acting alone, without sanction from David? I don't want to believe that David knows what's happening, but warning bells are clamoring for attention in my gut. I've felt something is off in this place ever since I arrived, and this only confirms it.

I pace back and forth, brow furrowed, unsure what to do, where to go. I can't just go back to my bungalow and go to bed now, hoping and praying Steps will be ok in the morning. *That's crazy, Reagan.*

I have to find and talk to David, tell him what I walked into. Then I'll know. If David is unaware of what Elder Allen is doing, well... he'll know now. If he is aware, then I'll have some of my questions about him answered, once and for all.

X

make my way back to the Commons, wincing when I hear a band playing a joyous gospel song. My mind flashes to an image of Steps, tied and being beaten to a pulp in a basement. My eyes narrow, anger rising.

Entering the building, I see David, sitting near the band, tapping his foot while he chats with some members of the Flock. I'm just about to make a beeline in his direction when Connor steps in front of me, stopping me in my tracks.

"Reagan."

I glare up at him. "Get out of my way Connor. I need to talk to David."

He just stands there, like a towering wall of muscle, staring down at me. "Talk to David about what?" His tone is mild, but his eyes are anything but.

I lift my chin, straightening my spine. "That's between me and David. Therefore, none of your business."

Connor snorts, rolling his eyes and I bristle. He steps closer to me, and despite myself, I back up a half step. "If I were you, I wouldn't go talking to David about anything." His gaze is hard as he crosses his arms, and his threatening words tick me off, making me all the more determined to reach David and tell him exactly what I know and saw. The fact that Connor is trying to prevent me from doing that and clearly doesn't want David to know what's happening to Steps is all the confirmation I need that I'm making the right decision.

"Get out of my way Connor." I try my best to sound threatening in return, although I'm not sure I succeed. Deciding bravado is the best recourse, I elbow my way past him, smiling inwardly at his grunt of discomfort when I connect to a rib. *Take that buddy. You deserve all that and more.*

I feel a tiny twinge of conscience, but shove it aside. My attraction to Connor is unfortunate, and it's clouding my judgment. *He's not a good guy,* I remind myself. If he were, he wouldn't be trying to stop me from telling David about Elder Allen.

Stomping my way across the room, I reach David, who looks up at me inquiringly. "We need to talk," I blurt out.

He lifts a brow, his bright blue eyes crinkling at the corners as he gazes up at me. "Why, of course, Reagan. How about we step outside so we can chat with some privacy, hmm?" Swallowing hard, I nod in agreement. *No turning back now, Reagan.*

He stands up, then leads the way. I follow him as we exit the Commons, and glower at Connor as we pass by. He glowers back, but doesn't say anything. David continues walking toward the fields, and I glance around us as I trail behind him, nervous and on the look out for any Shepherds who may be within hearing distance.

Once we are some distance out from the Commons, David stops and turns to face me. "Now, what is it Reagan? You appear upset." The moon is full, shedding a bright white glow all around us, lighting up the sky almost as much as the sun during the day. I look up at David's face, noting his concerned expression. I have to believe he doesn't know about Elder Allen, but what if I'm wrong? His expression doesn't do anything to eradicate my sense of uneasiness.

Swallowing my fears, I bite the bullet and blurt, "Elder Allen is in the basement of the Pen, beating poor Steps to a pulp! Is this the kind of place you're running here? A place that beats people as punishment for breaking some arbitrary rule?"

I clap a hand over my mouth, my eyes wide. I really hadn't intended for it all to come out that way. Dropping my hands to hang down at my sides, I straighten, gazing at David warily, and wait for him to respond.

He takes a moment, presumably to gather his thoughts, before he sighs heavily and shakes his head. "Reagan, you must be mistaken. I simply can't believe this. Elder Allen is a well-respected member of this community. He's a strong leader, one all the Shepherds look up to. I can't imagine him doing such a thing. We have rules and protocols to follow, however beating members of our community is certainly not one of them."

I stiffen, and glare up at him, not liking the implication of his words. "I know what I saw, David. Come with me, I'll show you."

David nods, his expression inscrutable. "Alright, please, lead the way." He holds out a hand for me to step ahead of him, and he falls in line behind me. We make our way back through the field in the direction of Shepherd's Pen without another word spoken between us.

When we reach the Pen, we enter and I can immediately tell the Pen is now empty. I can't see the light creeping up through the floorboards like I could before, and it *feels* unoccupied.

I make a beeline for the door that leads to the basement, eager to prove to David I'm not wrong, but knowing in my gut somehow, there will be nothing there to provide that proof.

I wrench the door open and flick the light switch, so that light floods the underground room. I clamber down the stairs, and as I expected, the room is empty. The wooden structure Steps had been hanging from is there, but there's no sign of him or Elder Allen, or any sign they'd been there at all.

David follows me down the stairs, and we both search the basement, but there is nothing. My jaw tightens with indignant anger. I turn to face David, and his gaze meets mine. He lifts his brows silently.

"I know what I saw," I say hotly. I feel tears of frustration well up, and blink them back.

David raises his hands up in a soothing gesture. "Calm down, Reagan dear. I'm sure there's a simple explanation. Perhaps you were mistaken. Why don't we go back to the Commons, and we can get this sorted out once we find Elder Allen?"

I cross my arms and glare at him. "I wasn't mistaken." I glance around the empty room then give him a grudging look. "But okay... let's go back to the Commons. Obviously Elder Allen isn't here."

His eyes get that ever present crinkle in the corners, and his lips lift in an actual smile this time. But somehow, it still doesn't feel as though the smile is genuine. He tilts his head in the direction of the stairwell, and I stomp past him. My lips twist. I know what I saw, and somehow, I'll prove it. *I'm just not sure how yet.*

Once we get back to the Commons, my eyes are drawn immediately to Steps and Elder Allen, sitting at one of the tables with a few other members of the community. My eyes widen, and I stop in my tracks. I grab for David's sleeve as he walks past me, and point in their direction.

David nods. "See? We'll get to the bottom of things here and now."

Yes, I think to myself. *Let's do that.*

We make our way over to the table Steps and Elder Allen are occupying, and Elder Allen looks up as we approach with a feigned look of surprise on his face. My stomach rolls in a somersault.

"Why David, Reagan, good evening!" he says with a jovial smile I can tell is forced. "How has the day fared for you?" He glances at me, and I shiver inwardly at the coldness in his gaze.

David clears his throat before speaking. "Elder Allen, the day has been good, thanks. Reagan here however, has brought some news to my attention that we need to resolve. Can you tell me where you have been the past hour or two?"

Elder Allen frowns. "Why, Steps and me here, we were simply off in a counseling session after dinner. Steps has had some recent struggles. Now he's repented for his sins though, and all is well." As he speaks, he slaps Steps on the back in apparent camaraderie, while his gaze meets mine.

Steps grimaces, and I cringe inside with him. Fury stirs, and my eyes snap to David. "You're not actually buying this bull, are you? I *saw* them, in the basement," I insist. "Look, it should be simple enough to prove. Lift his shirt, let me see his back." I point to Steps, who is sitting quietly, staring at the floor.

David and Elder Allen both glance around the room, and David says, "Please Reagan, might you lower your voice until we get this resolved? Elder Allen, why don't we head off to a more private area, and we can discuss this further. Steps here can show us his back, and all of this can be put behind us."

Elder Allen nods in agreement. "Sure, no problem, David. That sounds fair enough."

I step back with an expression of satisfaction, certain now that Elder Allen won't be able to refute the welts on Steps' back once they are revealed.

David motions to Steps, and before we can head off away from the crowd, Steps speaks up. "Please, David, sir. Really, I'm fine. Reagan must be mistaken in whatever it is she thinks she saw. I have sinned, and I'm very sorry. I've repented and I would just like to move on from the whole situation now."

Steps avoids my gaze as he speaks, keeping his eyes on the floor. He glances up at one point, and I can see the pain written on his face, but I can also see he's determined not to provoke Elder Allen any more than he already has.

My shoulders slump. Impotent anger bubbles in my chest, and I feel helpless. If Steps isn't going to speak up, I can't prove anything to David. I squeeze my eyes shut, shaking my bowed head at the floor in disgust.

"Steps, son, are you sure?" David asks. "We can go somewhere and talk privately if you prefer." David's eyes are bright, his expression friendly, while Elder Allen stares at Steps impassively.

The boy shrugs. "Yes sir, I'm sure. This has all been my mistake. I've sinned, and I'm very sorry for my actions. I would just like to finish dinner now and call it a night."

David nods. "Very well. I would like to finish my own meal as well. Elder Allen, join me?" Elder Allen nods, standing and giving a slight bow. "With pleasure, David." He shoots a glance my way, his expression smug.

David looks at me too. "Reagan, please, get some dinner and enjoy the rest of your evening. We will consider this matter resolved."

I stand there, my mouth hanging open.

The two of them head off. Steps avoids my gaze, turning back to his meal.

I close my mouth and look around, realizing everyone is staring at me. I glare at a few of them, and those closest all turn and get back to what they were doing before.

My eyes collide with Connor's across the room, and he just shakes his head, a look of irritation and disgust on his face, before presenting his back.

My lips tighten, and I spin on my heel, stalking to the exit to head back to my bungalow. *This night just couldn't get any better.*

XI

My eyes open to morning sunlight streaming through the window, and I yawn. My sleep was fitful, plagued by dreams that didn't make any sense. I rub my eyes tiredly, and drag myself to a sitting position, scrubbing a hand through my hair. Andie is already up and out, and I can't blame her.

Everyone in the compound was at the Common's last night. They all saw my confrontation with Elder Allen and David. I grimace and slide off the edge of the bunk, dropping to the floor. *Better get ready for breakfast, Reagan. Can't hide out here forever.*

As I walk across the grounds for breakfast, an announcement blares out over the compound's old-fashioned P.A.

system. "Attention all. Tonight there will be a special gathering in the Commons to address some community concerns. Please make sure you are there on time so we can get started right away." I don't recognize the voice, but I can guess what the meeting is about.

I sigh and glance around me. The formerly friendly faces of the Halcyon community now regard me with suspicion, a few even displaying outright hostility. I lift my chin and continue toward the Commons. Let them look.

When I arrive for breakfast, Andie and Robbie are already eating. I make my tray and then make my way to their table, taking a seat next to Andie. "Hi guys." They look up at me, but neither respond. I pause before asking, "So, has anyone seen Steps this morning?"

Robbie grunts then gets to his feet, picking up his tray. "Steps is resting, and wants to be left alone." He stalks off, tossing his tray in the trash on his way out the door. I stare after him for a moment in surprise, and then look to Andie. For the first time since I arrived here, cheerful Andie looks annoyed.

She tosses her hair over her shoulder. "Reagan, why would you want to come here, to this perfect place with people who have opened their doors and arms to you, and cause problems? I just don't get it."

My jaw drops at the same rate my anger rises. "Excuse me? Andie, this place is *not* perfect. Open your eyes, are you *blind*? I wasn't lying about Steps last night. He was brutally *beaten*, Andie... all for squirreling away some food. Freakin' food!" I exclaim, throwing up my hands. I glance around us and grimace. I don't mean to draw any more attention to myself I already have.

Andie's face turns pink, and she shakes her head, her expression stubborn. "No, you're wrong, Reagan. Steps even said he was just at counseling last night with Elder Allen, and nothing untoward at all happened."

She stands up, picking up her own tray as Robbie did moments earlier. "You know Reagan, you have just been *looking* for reasons to naysay this place ever since you got here. I don't know what your problem is, but maybe you're just so messed up by the outside world that you can't accept anything good in your life. You don't even know good when you see it."

She sniffs, tossing her hair again. "I don't know why you would ever want to live in a world like that, but I know I certainly *never* want to." With that, Andie spins on her heel and leaves me sitting there, staring after her.

I finish my breakfast slowly, keeping my head down to avoid the looks from all the people talking and eating. Then I make my way to the Pen and put on my uniform, getting ready for patrol. As I get ready, I mull the events of last night over in my head for the millionth time.

I know what I saw. I'm not crazy, and the worst part is, I'm starting to wonder who else knows what Elder Allen did to Steps last night, and just doesn't care. My thoughts linger on Connor, and I shake my head. No way could he know something like that and not do anything about it. I hesitate, staring at my shoelaces. *Says who, Reagan? You don't even know the guy.*

Still, some part of me senses instinctively that Connor isn't like that, that he has integrity. He wouldn't just stand by and let something so terrible and unjust happen, at least not without a very good reason. I finish lacing my shoes, and make my way to the main room. It's empty, so I take a seat to wait for the others to arrive.

The minutes tick by, and as the time to meet and head out on patrol comes and goes, the other Shepherds are nowhere to be found. I tap my foot, looking out the window outside to see if I see anyone. I don't, so I get to my feet and make my way to the door. I'll just follow the general route we took yesterday, and see if I run across anyone.

I walk quickly, not stopping this time to wave or say hello to anyone. It's clear the Flock members regard me now with mistrust and downright animosity, rather than friendliness. As I approach a wooded area, Terrence appears from within the trees, and he yells and waves his hands wildly, motioning for me to come help.

My instincts to assist override my sense of caution and I break into a run, following where Terrence disappeared into the woods. As I enter the trees, I'm immediately grabbed by both arms and yanked to a stop. My heart leaps into my throat and I almost choke on a scream. I start struggling, then hear a curse in a familiar voice.

"Calm down, Reagan," Connor growls, and I still, looking from left to right, my heart thudding loudly in my ears. He's gripping one arm, Laney is gripping my other, and both of their expressions are grim.

I blink in confusion. "What's going on?"

Elder Allen appears from the trees and approaches, and I feel the color drain from my face as I realize what's happening. He strolls toward us, his expression just as smug as last night, and Terrence follows along behind him, giving me an apologetic look.

"Reagan. Good morning. I trust you slept well. I know I did." Elder Allen smiles, and I feel a shiver ice its way down my spine once more. The man is just creepy. My eyes narrow, and I straighten, jerking both of my arms out of Laney and Connor's grip while glaring at them. Then I stand, chin up, as I wait for Elder Allen to get closer.

I don't answer him though, and his eyes harden. "Reagan, I'm sure you're wondering why you've been brought out here. It's pretty simple. Tonight, there will be a community meeting. At this meeting, David is going to offer you once again, two choices." His lips thin, and he glances at Connor and Laney before looking back at me.

"Choice one will be to stay on the island, learn to live by our rules and ways, and remain a member of our Flock as a Shepherd, as David believes is your divine providence." He pauses, then continues, "Choice two will be to take a boat back to the States tonight, and forget about this place. In return for which, we will simply forget about *you*." He glances down at his fingertips, picking at one of them before looking back up at me. He smiles, his eyes cold.

"You are strongly advised to accept the second option, Reagan. I do hope you won't disappoint us, like you did before."

Terrence and Laney exchange looks, and I glance at Connor. His face is impassive, but something flickers in his eyes. I swallow hard, and look back at Elder Allen. My body is vibrating with fury, but caution warns me that to react now would be folly. I glare at him, and he tips a finger to his hat.

"Until tonight." With that, he strolls off, and the three Shepherds fall in line behind him, casting me looks over their shoulders. Except Connor. He doesn't even look at me. They leave me behind to contemplate my decision, and I stare after them for a long while, watching as they become nothing but specks in the distance. When I can't see them any longer, I crumple to the ground, sobs escaping my chest as fear finally hits me.

XII

When night falls, I make my way to The Commons. The entire community is gathered there to hear David speak. I slip inside and stay to the back of the room, behind everyone, trying to remain as unnoticed as possible.

Then David begins to speak, and I stiffen. "Friends, members of the Flock. Tonight we are here because I'd like to tell you a little story. A little story about Reagan, our newest addition here on the island, whose only real crime in this world was in trying to do the right thing."

He goes on to tell everyone there my entire story, about Claire, about my being sentenced for a crime I didn't commit. He tells everyone that he believes God has placed me on

Halcyon so that I could walk a different path in this world, but that in the end, it's up to me to *choose* that path.

David then looks to where I'm standing against a back wall, and I shrink into the shadows as everyone turns to face me. "Reagan... thank you for coming. Please, join me here at the front." His blue eyes burn brightly in the light of the Commons, and I hesitate, glancing around at the sea of faces. Seeing no other option, I make my way slowly through the crowd to David's side. He places a hand on my shoulder and turns me to face the room.

"Members of the Flock, Reagan here has two choices, and I want her to know that we fully support and will love and respect her, no matter what decision she makes."

He then turns me to face him, placing both of his hands on each of my shoulders, and looking me in the eye. "Reagan, we would like to know which option you choose... stay here on Halcyon Island with all of us, and embrace your role of Shepherd, as one who will watch over and protect this Flock."

He pauses, and looks around the room, before back at me. "Or, take a boat back to the States tonight, and forget about Halcyon Island. If that is your choice, we will of course, pray for you and wish you God's speed."

He removes his hands from my shoulders, and laces his fingers behind his back, waiting for my response. I swallow hard, looking at his earnest expression, before glancing around the room. My eyes collide with Elder Allen's, and behind him, the gazes of all the other Shepherds.

I shift on my feet, feeling sweat bead its way down my back. I know that if I stay, Elder Allen is either going to make my life very hard, or very short. Not that it's ever really been easy. My lips twist ruefully.

My gaze roams the rest of the room, landing on Andie who is standing next to Steps, and my heart warms with affection. Even though I know she's mad at me, I can't help regarding her like a younger sister.

And poor Steps, he still looks as though he's in quite a bit of pain. I just know, down in my gut, that if I leave this place tonight and leave them behind, something terrible is going to befall them all.

I straighten my spine, and turn to face the crowd, before speaking in as confidant a tone as I can muster.

"David, thank you. Even though recent events have made things somewhat... challenging... I have not changed my mind. My choice is to stay here among all of you, and be a Shepherd. To help protect this Flock from any dangers that appear." My determined gaze locks with Elder Allen's cold one, and his eyes narrow.

Breaking contact, I muster a smile, and beam it out at everyone. David smiles too, standing next to me, his blue eyes doing their crinkle thing as a look of satisfaction crosses his face. The Shepherds all regard me with solemn expressions, as joyous gospel music begins to ring out and the Flock starts dancing and singing away any doubts they may have had about me.

I have to hand it to David, his followers really seem to go along with everything he says, without a peep of protest or angst. I make my way back into the crowd, and attempt to enjoy myself after the stressful night and morning I've had. Most of the Flock is very friendly and welcoming again, although there are a few that seem more distant than before.

Andie comes up behind me, putting her hand on my shoulder, and I turn to face her. Her expression is contrite. "Reagan, I'm really sorry for blowing up at you this morning. I don't know what came over me, this place isn't supposed to be like that. We're supposed to be better here than that sort of thing, and handle situations with grace and forgiveness."

I offer her a warm smile and throw my arms around her neck in a hug. "No worries, Andie. I'm just glad that we can get past it and move on. You're my closest friend here, I'd hate to lose that."

Andie brightens, and teases me. "I think I'm your *only* friend here at this point." Then her eyes widen, "Oh my gosh, I'm so sorry. That was so rude, I don't know why I said that."

I bust out laughing. "Andie relax. It's fine. You're probably right. Hopefully with time though, everyone here will come to accept me." I smile, and Andie nods, although she still looks embarrassed.

"Oh, before I forget. Connor said to tell you that David would like to see you in his office for a few minutes."

I frown, but nod. "Okay, I'll do that now." Andie grins at me, gives me another hug, and then wanders off to find Robbie.

I glance around the Commons, warning bells clanging in my head. I'm feeling overly cautious after this morning, but the Shepherds all seem busy with conversation and interacting with the Flock, no one appears to be missing.

I relax somewhat and make my way across the room to the exit, passing Andie and Connor as I do. I overhear Connor thanking Andie for delivering that message for him while he tended to Flock business, but I don't linger to hear Andie's response.

I make my way to David's office, glancing behind me every so often to make sure no one is following me. No one seems to be, so I relax a little more, but I can't shake the niggling sense of unease.

I knock on the door to David's office, but don't get a response. I listen, straining my ears to see if I hear anything, but there's only silence. I reach down to twist the knob, and it turns easily. Stepping inside, I glance around the office. "David?"

The door slams shut behind me, and Elder Allen's voice sends chills along my spine. "You should have taken that boat ride, girl." Then taking advantage of the element of surprise, he shoves me against the wall. He's fairly strong for a 60 something old man, and my head cracks against the wood, while pain shoots through my skull, dazing me.

He presses against the back of me, growling in my ear, "It's divine will that the people of Halcyon be protected, both from themselves, and from folks like *you*. Without those like me, people like Steps wouldn't survive this world of depravity long enough to be made *worthy* of God's love."

He spins me around to face him, and then backhands me. I stumble and fall against David's desk from the force of the blow. My ears ring and then my instincts take over as my head clears. I kick out at him in defense, just missing his groin but hitting his leg pretty hard. I give a grunt of satisfaction, my anger overriding caution.

Elder Allen snarls, losing his footing for a second, before rushing me and using his weight to press against me, pinning me to the desk. Self-preservation kicks back in and my eyes widen in fear as I struggle against him, trying to get free. His eyes are lit with something terrifying, and within seconds, his hands are wrapped around my throat and squeezing as hard as he can.

I swing my fist, aiming at his head, fighting for air. One arm scrambles behind me, frantically feeling around for the intercom button I know is there. It's the only thing I can think of to try and call for help. Finding it, I push it, doing my best to keep my finger on it so the transmission broadcasts while I struggle to fight him off.

Elder Allen is maniacal, spraying fury and spittle into my face as I choke, gasping for breath. He rants about fire and brimstone, and how I'm moments away from experiencing it firsthand, but his words keep fading in and out as I'm forced to go longer and longer without air, so much so that they begin to make no sense. *If they ever did.*

I bat weakly against his arm and face with my free hand, the finger of my other hand slipping from the button and then finding it again. I'm running out of steam as my body depletes of oxygen.

My vision starts to go black, and just as it does, I hear a voice barking, "Just *what* is going on in here?"

David. Thank you, God. Relief floods me as Elder Allen drops his hands from my throat like I'm on fire, and spins around to start stammering out an explanation to David.

I slump against the desk, holding my aching throat and sucking in huge lungfuls of air as my head and vision begin to clear. I cough, wincing at the pain. My heart thunders erratically, and my body shakes from the adrenaline surging through me.

David holds up a hand, stopping Elder Allen's nonsensical explanation in its tracks. His expression is formidable, one I haven't yet seen from him as he stares at us both. He glances down at my finger as it slips off the intercom button, cutting the transmission. Elder Allen follows his gaze and his face pales.

"Relax. It's all over now," David soothes me. He helps me stand up straight, and then lifts my chin, examining my throat, his charismatic blue eyes unreadable. "You'll need to get our nurse at the Pen to check you out, make sure there's no permanent damage."

I nod, it's all I can manage at the moment. Even swallowing is painful, never mind trying to speak. My chest heaves, and I sway as a wave of dizziness hits me. David catches me as I slump toward him, and he props me up. "Easy. Easy, take your time. Get your bearings."

I take a few more minutes leaning against him as the dizziness fades, before I straighten. Elder Allen is standing quietly, his head down, staring at the floor. Just the sight of him makes me sick.

"Come. The others will want to know what's going on," David states. He motions to Elder Allen. "You first."

Elder Allen doesn't say anything, just turns and makes his way to the door, his shoulders slumped forward. David helps me along and we follow behind him, stepping out of David's office into the small crowd waiting outside. Several members of the community are gathered, contained behind Connor, Laney, and Terrence who are watching the proceedings intently.

Connor stiffens when I step out and my gaze meets his, and I see something flash in his eyes, but I'm too exhausted to try to decrypt what it is. The man thoroughly confuses and infuriates me.

I hear rumbles of unrest from many members of the community as they begin asking what's going on, what happened.

David raises his hands, quieting them, before announcing, "Dear members of the Flock, it's with great regret and sorrow that I inform you Elder Allen has strayed from the path. He's committed crimes against one of our own, and he will have to be contained until such a time as we can be certain he is once again ready to join the ranks of our community."

He looks to Connor, Laney, and Terrence, motioning them closer. "Please escort Elder Allen to the Shepherd's Pen and restrain him. Make sure he's not a danger to himself or anyone else. Connor, you will assume Elder Allen's role as Overseer for the time being." Connor nods, his expression grim as his eyes find and lock on me once more. Laney and Terrence exchange worried looks, but step forward to do David's bidding. The Shepherds begin to take Elder Allen away, and Connor never takes his eyes off me until he passes by, his expression impassive.

I shift uneasily. His stare coupled with the recent nightmare with Elder Allen doesn't bode well for my future on this cursed island.

David calls out to Andie, "Andie, could you please take Reagan to the nurse and have her checked out, and then accompany her to the bungalow so she can get some rest. I'm sure she will feel better with some company."

Andie nods and steps forward, wide-eyed, her face etched with worry. I offer her a reassuring smile, and then we make our way through the crowd in the direction of the Pen, both of us silent, both of us reeling in our own way from events of the past hour.

The crowd parts to allow us through, and I tip my head forward, allowing my hair to hide my face as we walk. I sigh heavily, my breath shuddering in my chest. I have to fight back a sob, delayed emotions catching up to me. I am *definitely* ready for a good night's sleep.

XIII

The next couple of days I spend mostly resting in the bungalow, with Andie checking in on me periodically and bringing me food. I don't really have the mental energy to face the members of the Flock right now, I just need some time to myself to figure things out.

David makes an announcement over the intercom about Elder Allen, informing everyone that he has suffered a mental break, and he's undergoing treatment. He will not rejoin the community until it's certain he is fully recovered.

Andie said that there's been nothing but whispers the last few days but the announcement did the job of calming down the Flock. She said that once David made that announcement, everything seemed to go back to normal. I snort. *Whatever that means.* This place is nothing close to normal.

I look up from my chair where I'm flipping through an old magazine to pass the time as Andie enters the room, carrying a plate of food for dinner. She sets it on the table in the corner, and I offer her a smile of gratitude. Then she flops down on her bunk with a loud sigh. "This has been the most stressful week *ever*. But I think things are finally starting to calm down."

She rolls over on her side, laying her head on her hands as she looks at me. I get up to grab the plate and settle back down to eat. I'm starving, and my throat is feeling much better so it's easier to get the food down. Bruises still look pretty nasty though. She watches me as I eat, and we sit in companionable silence.

Andie breaks it first. "I'm really sorry about all you've been through since you got here Reagan. Things are *not* supposed to be this way here, I just don't get what's going on lately."

I feel a rush of sympathy for her. She looks so forlorn and confused, like she's lost an anchor in her world and she's drifting. I can only imagine how hard it must be to grow up in a place like this. There's a dark underbelly to this island that's beginning to come to light, and I can tell it's scaring her and making her worry about the future.

Setting my plate aside, I offer her a reassuring smile and

some encouragement. "I'm sure things will get better soon, Andie. Obviously Elder Allen is very disturbed, but hopefully with the right treatment he can overcome it and things will get back to normal around here."

I keep my thoughts to myself on just how far beyond normal I believe this island really is. There's no need to cause strife between me and Andie at this point. She really is my only friend here, so I don't want to alienate her by criticizing the island and the things I know and suspect about this place.

Andie yawns sleepily, prompting me to yawn too. "Thanks for bringing me dinner. Why don't we both get some rest for the night? Things will look much better in the morning I'm sure." She smiles and nods, closing her eyes and stretching out.

I climb on the top bunk and stretch out too, staring into the deepening darkness for a long time before I finally pass out.

It feels like I'd barely closed my eyes when I'm awakened by two people yanking me from the bunk in pitch darkness. I open my mouth to scream and someone claps a hand over it. Struggling furiously, fear and anger giving me strength, the only thing I can think is, *Great, here we go again.*

Someone stuffs a rag in my mouth and tapes it in place, and a pillowcase is pulled over my head before I'm dragged from the bungalow, wriggling and fighting every step of the way.

Once I feel the outside ground beneath my feet, I make a break for it, attempting to run, but then I'm caught by what feels like multiple people. My fear ratchets up a notch, my heart skittering like a bird in my chest.

The Shepherds. It has to be the Shepherds. They've come to cull the wolf from the Flock.

I stumble, almost falling, and someone catches me, pulling me back to my feet and pushing me forward. The darkness is overwhelming, my breath coming hard and fast through my nose as my ears strain to pick up any sounds that might clue me in on what's going on. I grunt through the rag, but nothing intelligible comes out.

Fear ices along my spine, and I think back on the recent weeks and everything I've gone through since being sentenced that day at court. Tears well in my eyes, but I fight them back, lifting my chin stubbornly. Whatever my fate tonight, I will *not* let them see me cry. I can't help but wonder though if this is how things end for people like me, people who try to do the right thing. *Seriously, what's the point?*

I stumble again as my feet hit sand, and I'm jerked upright by a strong hand on my arm. I wince at the tightness of the grip. I realize we are on the beach now, nearing the ocean. I try not to panic with thoughts of what may be coming next. My mind flashes back to Claire, and everything that landed me in this mess in the first place, and I swallow hard. Regret fills me, and I silently begin praying.

God, I know you and I haven't been real tight lately, but I've tried to be a good person, to do good things. Please, if there's any way to get me out of this mess, now would be a good time to reveal it.

Just then I'm shoved forward, and I drop to my knees in the sand. A few seconds tick by, amping up my trepidation. Then the pillowcase is jerked from my head, and I'm staring up into Connor's bright eyes. *Silver*, I decide. I couldn't really tell the color that first night, but since then I've realized they are some weird grey/blue color, depending on his mood. Only now they look more silver.

I glance around us in the dim light of the half moon and realize we're at the exact spot where he found me on the beach that day I washed to shore.

Laney and Terrence are standing off to the side, along with a number of others I can't quite make out in the dark.

Connor squats down in front of me, and I glare at him through the rag in my mouth. He studies me for a few minutes, and I squirm uncomfortably, but refuse to look away.

I can't help noticing his muscular forearms and strong hands draped between us though, and mentally kick myself at the blasted attraction to the man I can't seem to shake. It's obvious now that he's *not* a good guy, not like I ever thought he was. My heart lurches in disappointment, and I scowl.

His lips twist as he continues staring at me, and something glints in his mysterious eyes. *Laughter maybe? Awareness?* I can't really tell, but it's not the usual impassive expression I've become accustomed to, so it throws me off balance.

"I'm going to remove the gag in a minute, but first I need to tell you some things, and I can't do it with the threat of you screaming hanging over me."

He gives me an apologetic look, and I'm certain my own is incredulous. *Connor looking as though he's sorry?* My eyes narrow, but I just nod, indicating I understand.

He gestures to those standing around us. "We've all been impressed with your guts since you arrived. You did a real number on Elder Allen a few days ago, and vice versa if the marks on your neck and face are anything to go by." His jaw tightens, and I think I see anger flash across his face, before it's gone.

"It was everything we needed to see for reassurance, and now we're fairly certain you weren't placed on the island by David himself."

I stiffen. *Placed here by David? Like a mole or something? Why would David need a spy?*

My brow furrows, and Connor reaches out toward me. I shrink back instinctively, and he grins. "Relax. I'm just going to remove the rag now. Okay?"

I still and nod my head, gazing at him warily. He reaches out and gently pulls the tape away from my mouth. I grimace and then spit the rag out, spitting into the sand to get rid of the bad taste left behind.

"Why would I have been placed here by David?" I demand.

"Long story," Connor states. "But it's a good thing that you chose to stay on the island when given the option to go, because you would never have been allowed to leave here alive."

My eyes widen as comprehension hits. "You mean, David would have killed me?"

Connor nods grimly. "Not himself of course, he would have had someone do it for him, but same result."

I'm still confused, and it must show on my face, because Connor stands up and holds out a hand to help me to my feet. I let him pull me up, brushing the sand off myself as I look around the small group, all staring at me with solemn faces.

Connor waves a hand around at all of them standing nearby. "Reagan, meet the Sect. We're a very small group of people within the Halcyon community, mostly young, a few older, who just want to leave this island for good, start new lives somewhere else, and not be persecuted for our choice. Members of the Sect have been plotting a way off for awhile now."

I look at Connor, the many things that have been

confusing me about him finally clicking into place. "So you're like their leader or something?" Connor nods. "Or something. Someone had to take the lead before our actions got us all killed, and it fell to me."

Laney and Terrence move closer, and Robbie walks through the small group, appearing next to them where I can see him. Then Andie appears from the midst of the tiny crowd and I stare, my jaw dropping. "Andie?"

She runs up to me and gives me a hug. "I'm sorry, Reagan, I know we frightened you after everything you've already been through. I honestly had no idea the Sect even existed." She shoots Connor a glare, and he flushes.

"We didn't really know if Andie was ready to know the truth about Halcyon yet. She's been pretty attached to this place. But your arrival and then all the subsequent events...," he shrugs. "It all forced me to bring her in on things sooner than I'd planned. Right after Elder Allen was outed for the maniac he is." He scowls, grim satisfaction in his eyes.

I scrub my hands over my face, my emotions in turmoil. Then a thought occurs to me and I look over at Connor, horrified.

"You mean you've *known* what's been going on here, and you went along with it, even after what that psycho did to poor Steps?" My voice rises on the last part, and Connor puts a finger against my lips, cautioning me to be quiet. I slap his hand away, but my lip tingles where his finger touched me.

He grimaces, looking contrite. "When we initially saw Steps leaving the woods after storing food that day, we had no choice but to confront him about it. We had no way to know whether you were there to report us and our activities to David, or not. We couldn't take the risk. Steps took one for the team, so to speak."

They all exchange looks, and Connor continues, "In fact, everyone's behavior since you arrived has been because we were so afraid David had gotten wise to the Sect's formation, and we were worried he'd brought in someone to infiltrate us."

Laney pipes up, "Yeah, and then when you were placed in with the Shepherds, we had no idea *what* to think. It only seemed to confirm all our fears." Robbie and Terrence nod in agreement.

Connor continues with the story. "Then, that night with Elder Allen, he'd instructed me have Andie send you to David's office. I had no choice but to obey in order to maintain our cover, and I was in the process of working out what to do next, when the P.A. System started broadcasting Elder Allen's madness to the entire Flock. *Genius*, by the way."

He grins, his teeth flashing white in the dark. I stare

dumbfounded, realizing this is the first time I'd really seen him smile. It feels like a punch in the gut, and I close my eyes for a minute, trying to get my bearings with all of this new information, never mind my mixed feelings and unwanted attraction to Connor.

"So... if Elder Allen is now out of commission, why do you still want to leave? Isn't the problem solved?" I remember what Connor said about David and what would have happened had I chose to leave the island, but still find it hard to comprehend.

Connors lips tighten, and his expression grows grim. Laney and Terrence's expressions harden as well.

"Elder Allen is just the bulldog," Terrence interjects. "The bulldog's master is the rabidly insane David. He's a religious fanatic, and we're all in incredible danger the longer we remain here. I mean, level ten kind of danger, you really have no idea."

I think back to what I know of David, and all the small moments since I arrived where something about him has made me uneasy. Now I know why. My lips twist. *Good going Reagan. At least your instincts had recognized the crazy.* Even if my conscious mind didn't.

I look up at the stars, and they remind me to send a mental thank you to God for revealing the truth in all of this mess. *And at least your not dead*, I console myself.

I glance around at the small group, my eyes resting on

each one standing in a half-circle around me. I study Andie, and I can see the worry written all over her face, and the sadness. This is hard for her, I know. *And it really ticks me off.*

My gaze roves over the rest of the bunch before I lock eyes with Connor. In that instant, my decision to help however I can is made. *Come what may.* "So what's next then?"

They all look around at each other, and then back to me. Connor smiles grimly. "Next? We get the hell off psycho island."

Escalation (The Island II) is coming soon!

If you enjoyed Desperation, subscribe for updates:

http://www.cbstonebooks.com/subscribe-for-updates

Please keep reading for an excerpt from:

Rehabilitation (Unbelief Book I)
http://www.cbstonebooks.com/book/rehabilitation/

—

AN EXCERPT FROM CHAPTER I OF

REHABILITATION

The world's changed. I don't know this because I witnessed the change, or even because I felt it. No. This is all I've ever known, but I know it's changed because I see what's left behind.

Destruction.

Jacob is striding ahead of me, his strong back broad and straight, his steps sure and true. I often imagine he's balancing the world on those shoulders. His unruly blond hair is brushing past the nape of his neck, and I know his ice blue eyes are laser focused as he makes his way through the rubble. He's quiet, as am I, every step stealthy because though we know there aren't any people out here anymore, there are other things.

Dangerous things. We pick our feet up as we walk and make sure not to kick any of the debris surrounding us on accident. I grimace, eyes scanning the ground looking for anything that might be of value. The pack I carry slung across my shoulder is light at the moment, but I'm hopeful we'll be able to find something useful today.

Ahead of me, Jacob stills. He lifts a hand, signaling me to stop, then drops to his knees, crouching. I immediately follow suit, making myself as small and insignificant as I can, so whatever he's spotted, won't spot *me.* After several slow, quiet moments, hearing nothing but the sound of my breath as it clouds the air in front of me, I shuffle closer to Jacob.

"What is it?" I whisper in a voice quiet enough I don't think it'll carry beyond us.

He inclines his head in the direction in front of us. I squint, eyes searching along the cold terrain for the threat spurring us to crouch down out of sight. At first, I don't see much beyond the norm. There isn't anything visible other than the ruins of the Old World city. Then I catch movement out of the corner of my eye. I didn't notice it before, because its coloring matched the gray landscape around us, but now I see what has us stopped.

"A cougar," I mutter. The hairs on the nape of my neck rise and I suppress a shiver.

The large animal's gray fur looks mottled, missing patches here and there, striped by burns in others. It looks skinny, no doubt starving as are most things in the Old World. But I don't need telling to know its teeth work just fine, regardless of its meager appearance.

And its claws.

We wait in silence, holding our breath and watching the mangy animal limp and sniff at the air. After a while, it finally decides it's not going to find food or water is area and lumbers off.

We wait a few minutes more for it to disappe view before we straighten back to full height. I shrm shoulders as I do, trying to loosen muscles gone tight nerves. I expel a puff of air, it's smokey tendrils drifting toward the sky like a lazy feather. "Guess it didn't find an thing good out here," I mumble, then look over at Jacob unable to hide the relief in my tone or my face. "We got lucky."

Jacob looks down at me, a small smile on his face. "Luck has nothing to do with it." He winks.

I roll my eyes and start moving, passing him before he takes the chance to start this conversation again. Maybe if I just ignore him, he'll get the hint and won't start babbling on about fate and what not.

"Don't roll your eyes," he chastises, his voice carrying with it a gentle laughing tone as he follows behind me. "It's true."

Apparently, I am wrong about his babbling. I sigh. It

doesn't matter if keep walking or not, he's *still* going to bring it up.

"Can't we just keep moving?" I ask, my voice reflecting irritability / try to derail the subject. But Jacob isn't to be sidetrack

"W.e moving," he reminds me, laughter still coloring his ...ich is true, we are, but that isn't the point. I meant moving, as in no talking to accompany it. I sigh again, small crease indicating I'm cranky appearing between my brows. But Jacob is Jacob and he'll keep instigating this conversation--no matter how dangerous it is--because it's the type of man he is.

That's how much he... well, how important it is to him. I frown, a part of me proud he's so firm in his beliefs, another part worried it will get him in trouble one day.

"Think about it, Sinna," he tells me, and I can hear the excitement in his voice. "What were we doing the first time we met?"

I try not responding. Instead, I scan the area, looking for potential places that might hide things we can use or trade when we get home. It's the main reason we're out here anymore anyway, but it isn't the first reason we came into the ruined city.

"We were looking for a--"

"There!" I point ahead of us, not caring I just interrupted him. In the distance, maybe a mile away, there's a long building, the space of several Old World houses, and it's about the height of three of them piled on top of one another.

Jacob looks, bright eyes filled with hope as they search. Too late, I realize how my exclamation must have sounded to him. Sure enough, when he spots the building, his shoulders slump a little in disappointment and he lets out a sigh.

"--a church," he finishes. "We were looking for a church."

I feel guilty for getting his hopes up. Although we go out mostly now to find Old World items we can trade, Jacob still can't resist keeping an eye out for that fabled church.

"There aren't any left Jacob." My voice is quiet as I rest a gentle hand on his arm. "They were all destroyed after the War."

He only nods. I know he still dares to hope one survived, even though he knows the truth. I'm convinced that's why, out of everything the Elite has banned since the War, *belief* is most dangerous in their view.

You'll do crazy things for what you believe, even when you know what you're doing is pointless.

"Let's go," I tell him.

In perfect sync, we start moving toward the large building. I'm not sure what it is--maybe a school or a prison perhaps. Those are the buildings we find most often, and most of the stuff inside them is deteriorated beyond any recognition or value. But every once in a while we we get lucky and find something good.

Personally, I hope it's a hospital we're walking toward.

Hospitals always hide the good stuff. Drugs, antibiotics, and other medical things most people back home don't possess and can't get. A hospital would be best case scenario in my book.

"Maybe it's a library," Jacob muses out loud. His voice is still saddened, but he's trying to stay lighthearted and act as we always do on our trips into the Old World.

"A library," I scoff. "What about a hospital? Hospitals always have the best stuff." My words escape unthinkingly, echoing my thoughts of moments ago.

Jacob just shrugs. "Depends on what you're looking for I guess."

I roll my eyes at him again and we fall back into easy silence. Libraries are okay, I admit to myself. I'm not sure I'd ever let on to Jacob though. Books are rare and hard to get your hands on. The only people who can print them anymore is the Elite and most of those are so filled with propaganda (and are flat out boring, if I'm being honest), people just aren't interested in reading any of them.

But *Old World* books are a different breed altogether. They're filled with adventure, romance, and most dangerous of all (at least according to the Elite), Old World history. There's a market for such books, albeit a narrow one. First, only people who *can* and *do* read want them. That narrows down buyers considerably. Then you need to find people willing to take a risk they've gotten their hands on a banned book. The list given out by the Elite containing banned books you can't read is so long no one's real positive exactly what's on it. And to top it all off, you have to find someone who isn't going to turn you in if you sell them a book.

I know a few people who fit the profile, but they can't buy books often and are only on the look out for specific ones, so I don't much like making book runs.

Jacob's looking for a specific book, too. That's why he's so interested in the libraries. The thing is, the book he's looking for is *definitely* banned. It's the only one on the list that everyone knows it's illegal to have.

Worse than illegal in fact. Having it could land you in Rehabilitation. Or worse.

Secretly, I hope he never finds the book he's looking for. I don't tell him this, but in my heart I hope for it every time we leave the safety of home.

Please don't let him find it.

I've been in the lead, but Jacob takes over as we head toward the entrance. I can't help but feel slightly annoyed at him for putting himself ahead of me. It's not a jealousy thing. I know it's about protecting me, his going ahead, but it annoys me no end he thinks I need protecting.

Nevertheless, I follow him up concrete steps toward the set of double doors. Jacob pauses right outside them. There's a couple windows looking into the building, but they're narrow and dirty, covered in years' worth of dirt and grime. Inside, it's impossible to see a thing.

Jacob glances at me and raises his eyebrows in question.

"What do you think?" he asks me silently.

I hesitate.

Being out in the ruins of the Old World is dangerous for a lot of reasons, but the most pressing one right now is we don't know what's inside that building. It could house another wild cat like the one we saw earlier, or could be filled with toxic mold, or be ripe with some other unexpected danger.

When we get inside the building though, it isn't what either of us thought it would be. It isn't filled with poisons or dangerous predators--at least, from what we can tell--but it also isn't quite as exciting as we'd hoped. Instead, it's a school. For younger kids it looks like. At least that's what I think, based on the rotted and molding smiley faces plastered on the walls.

"So much for the hospital," I mutter, my voice echoing through the long hallway, sounding eerie.

Jacob shrugs and acts as though it doesn't matter, but I can tell he's disappointed, too. He was really hoping for a library. Or a church. I mentally sigh, my innate worry for him rising up again.

"There might still be something good," he says with a smile.

I shake my head at him, amused. "Ever the optimist."

Together we walk down the hall, our steps cautious. Debris taking the form of everything from bricks to shoes to scraps of old, shredded clothing litters the ground. We're treading lightly, because although it doesn't look like anything is here, we know better than to assume there isn't. I glance at the doors along either side of the hallway and cringe back, trying to put more distance between them and myself. There are large X's on some of the them. Both Jacob and I avoid these automatically. There aren't any history books that talk about the Old World and the Last War much, not in any detail at least, but we have been out here enough times we know exactly what's behind those doors.

And I have no desire to see it.

"Must have been close to one of the bomb sites," Jacob murmurs, as though afraid to wake the dead. Or maybe he's just showing respect. "My dad used to say that when the population got exposed to toxins from the bombs, a lot of people suffered. Some decided it was better to just... go out quietly instead."

Jacob's dad has been dead about as long as mine's been missing. I don't think they'd been friends or anything, but I think that if they'd gotten to know each other, they would have been. At home, neighbors didn't like mixing, it was too risky. Anyone could be an Elite hiding out, just waiting to make their move. The only people you can trust are your family members.

It was a fluke me and Jacob even became friends. And if I'd been older, like I am now, I don't think it would have happened.

I glance at him sideways, studying his strong profile as he stares at the X on one of the doors. I'm glad we met when we were kids... even if we can never to agree on much of anything.

Folding my arms across my chest, I mutter, not able to help myself, "Or this was a testing site, just like the Elite always says. How people used each other to test out new drugs, new weapons, not caring what happened to them."

Jacob looks back at me casting me a sharp glare. He has always hated the Elite--I do, too, if I'm being honest--and he's not afraid to say it either. Contradicting something his dad said in favor of something the Elite say... well, if it wasn't necessarily very nice of me, it was important to do. I lift my chin, my stubborn streak stirring to life as I glare back at him. He forgets sometimes we live in a world with specific rules and breaking them comes with dire consequences.

Besides, the world we're standing in right now is ruined. That's kinda the point. If they hadn't been awful, cruel people, why is their world obliterated, nothing more than X's on the doors to mark where their people died?

"Let's keep going," Jacob's tone is gruff, revealing just a hint of anger, so I keep quiet as I follow him.

When we decide the place is safe enough, we split up after finding a map on a wall. Jacob goes to the left toward the library (of course) and I go to the right, heading down the hall toward the nurses office.

I don't know if there will be anything there worth scavenging, but I figure it will still be my best bet. I pass at least ten doors with X's on them, and knowing each one of them holds a room full of bodies elicits an involuntary shiver as I walk. I can't help it, it just feels *creepy*. I know they're nothing but bones, mostly, but sometimes, if the room was sealed up tight... that's why we never check the rooms anymore. We go where we think there will be the best stuff, look around, and leave as quickly as we can.

The nurse's office is toward the back, near the big gymnasium that students used for physical activities.

Sometimes I wonder what it would have been like to go to a school like this... and then I decide it must have been terrifying. All those other kids, none of whom you could trust, and a teacher at the front telling you what to think.

I imagine it is a lot like Assembly. We have it every other day in the After World, usually, although less often as we get older. All of us, kids eighteen and under, gather in the courtyard in the middle of town and watch the large glass screen light up. Most of us can't read, so when the scrolling words travel across the glass there's a voice that accompanies it. It's always a bland, toneless man's voice. He lists off the three main rules that govern the After World.

Don't repeat mistakes of the Old World.

Don't seek love, don't engage in war.

And above all else, don't Believe.

There are other things after that, usually. An update on Rehabilitation camps, success stories and sometimes failed escape attempts. Occasionally we get news of political things, but politics are only for the Elite, so no one cares too much about those.

Most of us are more worried about surviving.

I reach the nurse's office to find it's mostly intact, only a few things obviously searched through. Some places look ransacked already when we get there, making me wonder if there are others who search the ruins like we do, or if people of the Old World were scavengers, too.

Pulling my bag off my shoulder, I start throwing things that look promising into it. Most of them, I don't know what they are or what they do, especially since most of the labels look deteriorated, but it doesn't really matter. People will trade for it anyway.

I stuff all of it in my bag, as much as I can fit, and I'm about to leave the room when I glance to my right and see something sitting on a desk. It's covered in a thick layer of dust, but it still catches my eye. I can only make out the words healing and prayer, but that's enough. My lips tighten, feeling a rush of gladness Jacob isn't with me.

I leave as quickly as I can and pretend I never saw the book at all. I meet up with Jacob further down the hall. He's found some books too--picture books in fact, which are great, because people will be more inclined to buy them since they don't need a lot of skill as far as reading goes.

"What did you find?" Jacob asks as we head out.

"Nothing," I answer automatically, mind recalling an image of the book I left behind again and again. I remember the words written on it.

Healing and prayer.

Eyes grim, I repeat again as we step out of the building to head home, "Nothing." Thankfully Jacob leaves it at that.

Continue reading Rehabilitation (Unbelief Book I)

http://www.cbstonebooks.com/book/rehabilitation/

AUTHOR SECRETS

HA... and there you are thinking I'm going to reveal big, dark, secrets. Sorry dear readers, not I, not this day. But I will share a few fun facts.

Ahem. ::Donning 3rd person hat::

C.B. Stone is sometimes called author, writer, or purveyor of stories. One might even dub her a yarn spinner, if you will. It's very possible she might be considered just a little left of normal by most, but she's cool with that. Really, she's too busy avoiding normal to care.

On any given day, you might find Stone pounding away at a keyboard in sunny Miami, contemplating waves, contemplating life, and dreaming up more exciting stories to share with readers. Except Sunday's of course. Sunday's are God's day, so you'll often find her making her best "joyful noise" with her local church praise team.

When not pounding poor fingers to bloody nuggets and reinventing the definition of eye strain, C.B. Stone enjoys living it up, doing the family thing, the kid thing, and the friend thing. And in her downtime, reading the minds of fans
.

Also being invisible. Being invisible is fun.

CONNECT WITH C.B. STONE

IF you liked Desperation, Book I in The Island Trilogy, make sure you like C.B. Stone on Facebook, and sign up via email for updates on upcoming books and release dates.

And if you're interested in opportunities for advance review copies of future books and/or being a beta reader, please feel free to send her a PM via Facebook expressing your interest, or if you sign up for updates via email, you can hit reply to any message and reach her directly.

Connect with C.B. Stone online:
http://www.Facebook.com/AuthorCBStone
http://www.CBStoneBooks.com
http://www.CBStoneBooks.com/Subscribe-for-Updates/

Note from the Author:
If you enjoyed reading Awakening, I would love for you to help me share this book with others who might enjoy it as well. You can do this in several ways.

Recommend it.
You can do this by recommending to friends and family, sharing it on social media, in readers groups, and on discussion boards.

Review it.

I'd love for you to tell others what you liked about this book by leaving a review on Amazon or Goodreads or both. I appreciate readers who take the time to leave thoughtful reviews of my books, so if you leave one, please be sure to email me at author@cbstonebooks.com so I can send you a personal thank-you. You can also contact me via my website at *http://www.CBStonebooks.com.*

Lend it.

I've enabled lending of this book if you downloaded the Kindle version from Amazon, so please do share with your friends. Thanks so much!